STEALING THE BOGEYMAN'S BRIDE

Faetales Novella #2

Poppy Minnix

ONE NIGHT READS

DEDICATION

To everyone who needs to angle their
book so passersby
don't catch a glimpse and
clutch their pearls so hard they
hurt their hand.

CONTENTS

INTRODUCTION

Note: In 2025 Poppy Minnix absorbed her alternate pen name Georgie Monroe (original author). The Faetales series will continue under Poppy Minnix

Hello readers of fantasy and spice!

This story is a 2-hour average read and has dark themes with high spice levels. It's book two in the Faetales series. If you haven't read book one, The Springfest Sprint, the characters and world in this story are introduced there. But if you'd rather just jump in or need a refresher, here's a quick breakdown to get things rolling...

- This spicy fae series is made up of short, fast-paced novellas (75-150 pages) that will link heavily story-to-story. Reading them in order will help with the quick pacing and overall storyline, though each can standalone.

- Book one, The Springfest Sprint, starred Princess Ember of the Seelie Spring Court, and Prince Typhon of the Unseelie Crown Court. They are heavily involved in this book.

- The Seelie are iridescent-winged faeries, small and delicate in stature. Most have magic abilities and some can create impressive glamours (see definition below). Seelie like to think of themselves as the good fae because they're kind to humans and other creatures, and they avoid conflict. But they have some dreadful traditions like The Springfest Sprint—a mate-claiming race for those who have come of age and haven't yet bonded with another, and arranged marriages with magical bonding instead of natural mate-bonding. They are possessive of what's theirs, including friends and mates.

- The Unseelie are another type of faery, though they're a little bigger, have bat-like wings, and a dark side that arises when they have intense emotions like fear, rage, or lust. That makes their eyes go crimson, their fangs drop, and shadows darken certain areas of their bodies, making their features appear sharper and more dangerous. Most of them also have a variety of magic abilities, and they're great at creating and taking down territory wards. They have rules of tradition when courting a mate, but are also typically polyamorous.

- Both types of fae have courts—kingdoms with kings and queens, princes, princesses, dukes, etc. They all have their own processes of ruling over their kind and keeping their territories organized.

  - Seelie courts: Spring, Summer, Autumn, Winter.

  - Unseelie courts: Crown, Northern, Enforcer, West Wind, Hillock.

- There have been and will be lots of different fae-folk mentioned along the way—sprites, Sidhe, pixie, leprechaun, Selkie, Boggarts, Brownie kin, kobolds, trolls, leshy, dryads, nymphs, and more. There is so much amazing lore on these fae beings and I'm inspired by some of that, but also create my own lore versions which will continue to build through the series.

- Time! The faeries don't use the human standard of time like minutes, months, and years. They use "flaps/flutters" for something like a second, "moon/moon cycle" for a month, and "full rotation/rotation" for a year. They use decade (10 rotations), century (100 rotations) and millennium (1000 rotations).

- Glamours are a vision some fae can cast to confuse or impress. They can disguise themselves as a character did in The Springfest Sprint and Faetales shorty, Go Ahead and Steal My Heart, create imaginary animals like snakes and rabbits, or create a full scene that an enemy could get lost in like a fake forest or cave. Some fae are better at glamours than others—Ember is a glamour-champion in The Springfest Sprint.

I hope that helps in getting you ready to jump into the action. One last thing! Flip the page if you don't like trigger warnings...

...

...

...

... Here goes ...

If you're not up for reading about a marriage of deceit, heavy mental and some physical domestic abuse, graphic and frequent sexual descriptions, and graphic violence, this is your warning!

Enjoy! Poppy

CHAPTER ONE

LOVE IS DUMB

AURALIA

As first advisor to the missing king, I made an oath to represent the Unseelie Crown Court with grace and dignity. Yet, here I am, hiding behind a castle curtain.

My earlier argument with Donovan over how to address the ongoing issue of our missing king got me worked up, and I might have flashed him as I stormed out of the meeting—subtly, of course. And then I've avoided him for the rest of the day, because I know better than to tease him. Or I don't, because I can't seem to stop.

Shame on me. Again.

From not far enough away, Jinora's tinkling laugh sounds more like a Seelie's, and I want to bite her tiny nose off.

His responding chuckle is carefree. Looks like she was available to soothe his irritation.

Clutching my shirt over my heart, I think about where he went since I toss him into a tornado of mixed signals daily.

Did they spend the day fucking their way through every position I know firsthand he's exceptional at? It's likely.

Did he look at her with sweetness? Carefully caress her because she's kind and gentle? Of course, he did.

I haven't experienced something like that with him. Frustrated moments of uncontainable lust make up our interactions, because I can't allow myself to fall further than I already have.

We've known of each other for a decade, but three rotations ago, I gave in to my wants and, unfortunately, being in bed—or against walls, doors, the castle wall, or behind curtains—with Donovan was far better than I'd expected. Ever since then, I've been fighting with myself to leave him be. Don't let him closer. *Don't put him in danger.*

Their muffled words sound like they're spoken against skin.

I dig my nails into my palms to distract myself from the images my brain supplies when I should conceptualize every detail of the perfect life Donovan and Jinora would have together. That is not our future, and I need to let him go. I need to get out of here before they wander even closer, and I overhear sweet words that will burn my charred heart further. He's not mine and never ever will be. *Stop this now, Auralia. Sneak away, go rescue your king and get back to upholding the will of the Unseelie Crown Court for as long as you can.*

Footsteps approach and an energy that is unmistakably Donovan's halts too close.

A shiver rolls up my spine.

The curtain opens with gusto.

Donovan's face is so beautiful. It's like looking into a perfect moon for too long and then being unable to see anything else in the darkness. With big brown eyes, dimples, and a square jaw—he's too much. His black curls look as if Jinora gave them a good tug when she came, and rage consumes me. However, his gaze is twinkling with mischief and

I'm very busted. He knows me well—or as well as I've allowed him to know me.

I grip the curtain fabric to shake it. "These are getting dingy. You should see to the maintenance as the stand-in king's second."

"Are you so bored that you're insulting the decor, pet?"

He knows I hate that nickname so much, but not why. I'll never confess, but now it's a game to him—one I created by my reaction. And when he wants to taunt me, he knows how.

I bare my teeth at him. "Better than insulting your choice of bedmates. Don't you think, little Donnie?"

His eyes narrow and he steps close enough that I'm surrounded by the heat of his powerful body and the scent of berried wine and cacao.

My mouth waters. I slip to the side.

He flattens a palm against the wall, blocking me in. "Are you insulting yourself, Aura?" His purring tone calls right to my nipples and my wings go hot. He traces a line over the sensitive membrane with his finger and smirks.

"I'm not your bedmate." I duck and spin out of reach. Letting go of him is at the top of my priority list and yet, right before I dart around the corner, I glance back at him and my eyebrows raise in question without thought. Stupid me, pretending this is a game when it's not. Why do I do this to myself? To him? It's not fair to either of us, but my life hasn't been fair for eleven rotations, and my shame still feels fresh. I was so reckless and young. So needy and trusting.

Yet my past has taught me nothing because I stupidly love Donovan Germanthia with everything I am.

I'll never show him that. Never say it. I can't.

Because I stupidly loved someone else first, and I betrayed the Unseelie kingdom for him in the worst way.

Chapter Two

LOVE IS PAIN

DONOVAN

Auralia shoots down the hall like a waving red flag, and it's on.

I follow the sway of her copper curls that lead to those luscious thighs and round ass. She's the most beautiful being I've ever seen. But when she gets like this—tense and territorial—I drop everything and follow. We may fight more than we fuck, but if there's an opportunity to find myself in her bed, I'm taking it.

Her deep gray wings tuck tighter, stretching the soft membrane over the peaks of the top knuckle. I smile, anticipating her next move, and make a leap for the hidden hallway before she does. We crash together, my hand on her hip and both of hers on my chest. I press her against the wall and lean close, melting into her cloudy-day eyes. "Jealous again, pet?"

I knew the slap was coming—she drops fangs when I use that nickname—but I didn't expect the kiss.

Her palm creates a sharp sting, then her lips deliver heaven as her taste greets my tongue, a sweet nectar that washes away the ash of her strike. She grips my tousled curls and I grin. Definitely jealous. I won't tell her I messed up my hair the moment I walked away from Jinora. If Auralia can be secretive, so can I, and I needed to know that our game is still on.

I suck Auralia's neck, when she moves her face to gasp for air, then grip her thighs to lift her so I can grind into her sweet heat.

She shoves me away.

I growl at her until I catch onto the footsteps and unfamiliar voices from far down the hall.

She wipes away my kisses like being caught with me would ruin her reputation for life. *Unbelievable.*

Cruel ways to insult her spin inside me. *I'm a catch for someone who's magicless.* That would be true if she wasn't so superior at everything else. And besides... although we're in equal positions, she's more respected than I am. It's one reason she's the king's right hand and I'm the prince's. I bring a little needed chaos to the royal party, where she's as rational as they come.

Even though we could slip farther into the blind passage and rut in narrow space, she turns from me and darts back into the main hallway.

"What the fuck, Aura?" I follow again, wondering why she's even cagier than normal. Was she expecting someone? Does it really embarrass her that much to be seen with me by visiting diplomarians? I doubt any of our people are unaware there's something fierce between us, even if most of our time together is behind closed doors and within hidden passages.

She straightens her shirt, glancing around the hallway like a wraith may pop out at any moment, and holds a palm against me when I move closer. "Leave me be."

I've tried, and that doesn't work.

Her blue-gray irises rim red when she glances at me one last time and heads down the hallway, away from the voices.

I follow. Unseelie have a dark side. A monstrous version that comes out to play when there's a threat or intense emotions. *Why this time, Aura?* I loop an arm around her waist, and get a sharp elbow jab, but it's her face when she spins that makes my breath freeze. Terror, stark and chilling, pales her dark honeyed skin, despite the deepening shadows around her eyes, on her cheeks, and sharpening her collarbones. She's losing it.

"What's wrong?" I lean toward her, wanting to cup her face and bring her back into my arms. Fear does not work on her features. I have to fix it.

She shakes her head and her nostrils flare as she shoves at me again, hard and desperate. "I don't want you near me. Leave me alone."

I wish she were lying, but that's not possible with the liar's curse on all fae.

The approaching voices quiet to mumbled whispers.

I pivot to see if the strangers are in sight, but the hallways are still clear. When I turn back, Auralia is gone. Closing my eyes, I breathe in the last wafts of her peppery scent mixed with our lust and hate. I torture myself with it for another moment, then go to meet whoever is roaming the halls, because if Auralia doesn't want them here, they're not welcome.

CHAPTER THREE

SITUATIONAL CRISIS TIMES TWO

AURALIA

My stomach roils. I had to be imagining that scent, right? I'm only getting the faint phantom whiff of plumeria because there are guests in the castle, and I'm always one step from panic when there are guests in the castle.

But it could be him.

Why would Bogen be back, though? He hates me as much as I hate him. Or I think he hates me. There's no way to tell.

Darting down the east corridor, I head toward the king's chambers.

Donovan better not follow me. Every time I'm forced to push him away, something inside me cracks. One day, I'm going to break into a pile of rubble, because I can't stop when it comes to him. Not laughing at his endlessly amusing wit has truly tested my acting skills. And when he touches me? He's impossible to ignore. I shouldn't have leaned into him that first time—it changed the simple tolerance we had for each other—but it was as if every cell inside me awakened and pulled toward him like a magnet. That still scares me.

I had feelings for Bogen too. Strong ones. And here I am, fangs descended, wings and muscles tense and ready to strike, though it's foolishly pointless. I can't harm my bonded mate. My stomach churns just considering it.

I peek into each empty room as I approach Kage's office—or maybe it's Typhon's now. My king accepted an invitation from the brand new Rioch nymph queen, then never returned, but his younger brother has acted as in his stead since we received the first prisoner correspondence eight moons ago. Though unprepared, Ty took over meetings and decisions, just as Kage took over when his father—I shake my head. I'm one step from flying out a window and screaming at the mountains. I need to gain back control, and thinking about the past won't help that one bit.

As soon as I barge into the king's office, my shoulders sink in relief.

"Why in the realms not?" Ember yells as she holds a parchment. Maybe I was a bit quick to be relieved. The Seelie princess, now our regent queen consort, has her dainty hand on her hip and her light, iridescent wings flit in irritation. They give the same buzz as when she's about to come, so it's hard to tell if she's truly livid or turned on. Especially when she can be both.

Though, as I check out her mate, it's got to be actual anger.

Typhon is red-eyed and shadowed. Our stand-in king rises from the desk chair, fists to the wood, looking dangerous, yet somehow princely. "Because they are threatening to kill any—"

"Unseelie," Ember yells back, throwing the paper down. She's about half his size and the only being who refuses to yield to him.

He growls. "Or those associated with the Unseelie courts. That's you, *mate*."

I'm not even sure they notice I'm here.

Crossing the room, I pick up the paper. It's the nymph queen's familiar scrawl, giving another refusal to release Kage. This excuse is a bit more fleshed out. They're keeping him for his guidance on their coven structure. It's a hard thing for a fae to admit weakness in their goings on. Odd to trap an unwilling Unseelie king for the job, though. She proclaims they will keep him for as many moons as it takes to make progress and to stop threatening them. What a silly request. They stole our king. They may have the intention of returning him eventually, but we need him too, and unless he sends instructions to leave him be, we're going to threaten.

I clap to stop the yelling and wave the letter in the air. "Is this why there are people in the castle?"

Typhon stretches out his gray wings as he straightens his back. "Yes. Three delegates came through—two from the Northern Court brought the letter, and an elder from the Enforcer Court wanted to express her concern. The trolls are infringing on territories, so I was expecting their visit any day."

Good. Not the trolls, but the visitors. We know them. They can be logged and tracked back. No strangers.

I fold the paper and set it on the desk. "I'll put together a response."

"No need." Ember turns to the door, still glaring at Typhon. "I will. In person."

"Not happening." Then Typhon is out the door after her. I sigh. They'll be fucking against the wall in less than five flaps, and if my mood was better, I'd possibly join in.

Sitting at the desk, I write out another letter to the queen of the Rioch coven. I tell her that her issues are her own and to release Kage immediately as she's gaining unsavory attention, possibly from the trolls. It's not a lie because if we can't control them, they'll be on the nymph's doorstep soon enough. No matter how many leshies and dryads they've attracted to protect them, there would be a battle death count. That may be enough of a threat to get somewhere. Fae do not like dying.

As I'm finishing up, there's a shuffle of fabric that brings my attention to the door.

Jinora steps in, putting a smile in place as if clipping on a necklace. Some days, I think she's as good of an actress as I am. "Have you seen Donovan?"

I narrow my eyes and return my attention to the letter. "Not for a few." *Moments.* "What do you need?"

"Nothing. I just wanted to..." She pauses long enough for me to look up. "*Talk* to him."

Do not rip apart and set fire to the letter, the desk, or Jinora. That would be unkind and draw attention. "I don't know where he is."

"Ah, well. I'll catch up with him soon enough." She taps the doorframe, bringing my attention to a massive line of bruises on the underside of her biceps.

"What happened?" I point to her arm. Does she have an angry lover that's as thrilled as I am about her hanging out with Donovan?

Her brows raise in surprise when she sees where I'm looking, and she rubs the spot as if it's charcoal. "Oh, that." She turns back to me with a smile and steps backwards into the hall, though holds her arm at an uncomfortable angle as if pressure on it may pain her. "Well, if you see Donovan, send him my way."

Never in a thousand rotations. "Jinora, why are you bruised?"

She puts her hand on her hip. "Aren't we nosy today? It's nearly dining time. Have a good evening, Auralia."

Before I can stop her, she's down the hall. Clearly, she doesn't want to talk about it. I'll let it go for now because I'm the last person who should try to pry open someone's secrets. Then they may take aim at mine.

I make a note for Typhon, telling him to check on Jinora, and her bruise, then head to my room. As soon as I open the door, a waft of familiar plumeria hits me in the face, and all the relief I'd found by thinking I was safe skitters away, replaced by a rod of tension in my spine.

Honey-blond hair frames the face I used to believe was the most gorgeous in the realm. Light gray eyes peer at me from under broody eyebrows.

"Release the glamour," I growl, though I'd rather run. This fake face brings memories I'd do nearly anything to forget.

Bogen's true face matches the ugliness of his soul.

He sucks his glamoured tongue against his top teeth and stands from sitting on my bed. "What a sour greeting for your husband. And on our anniversary too."

CHAPTER FOUR

NIGHTMARE ALIVE

AURALIA

I've learned much from this creature that is my bonded mate. Naivety can ruin so many lives and betrayal can make one physically ill. I've found out how much some creatures enjoy tasting fear.

If I show any emotions that go with those lessons, he will annihilate any calm I have left and happily turn me into a cowering shell of what an Unseelie can be. He's done it before. Too many times.

"Our anniversary, huh?" I sigh and walk to my dresser. I could never use my mother's dagger on him, but it's comforting to keep it close, nonetheless. "That's probably a lie. I thought I smelled you around, *husband.* How long has it been?"

He narrows the eyes of his glamour.

I hate that he uses this form. It reminds me of how much I wanted the fae he's imitating. How it never occurred to me to question why, after cycles of being ignored, Duke Cherune, my unrequited love, was wooing me. It's foul to remember how *honored* I was to finally kiss him and then be under him, taken by him until my world went to hell in one short afternoon.

"It's been a mere six moons, pet." He comes closer.

By the mystical bond we share, I should feel relief to be around my mate. But that part of our bond broke when he showed me his true face and I realized the fae I loved was an imposter.

Clenching my teeth, I keep my boots firmly planted on the floor. Running will only make things worse. "Hm. Isn't it a bit early for your catch-up visit?" It's usually a full rotation between his physical check-ins. He still has his minions, though. They leave notes from him in my pockets or under my pillow—places closest to me so I understand Bogen is always watching me and can show up in my room whenever he pleases. I cross my arms. "Why are you here this time?"

"Ah. My inquisitive *wife*." Moving close, he leans to inhale my neck, making my skin prickle. "You've been terribly naughty." He skims my arm with his knuckles.

Cringing, I pull away on instinct. "And how's that? I've only been here, doing my job."

He grins.

I'm in for it. I turn toward the wall. "Release the glamour. *Please*."

Chilled fingers grip my chin and jerk my gaze back to him. "But you like this form, pet. You love touching it and moaning for it like a nymph, though you're not nearly as skillful as one."

Hissing, I jerk my face from his hold. "That was different, and in the past. You deceived me."

"No less deceitful than what you've done. Confess."

"Confess what?"

There are a variety of things I've put into play to detach from him—and I hope he doesn't know about any of them—but it's more likely a trick. His way of baiting me into telling him anything I've been up to. That only worked for a short time early on, but he still tries. I prepare to run as he reaches into a satchel attached to his belt. But instead of a poisonous spider or hexed gem, he pulls out something far more terrifying because this time, I'm caught.

He pinches a familiar thick lock of my hair, dipped in my blood, and bound with wormwood and turmeric. "I'd wondered why you hadn't yet gone into heat, and was concerned that my investment was a dud." He pouts his too-familiar lips before grinning.

He loves to speak like the fae whose identities he steals instead of the Boggart that he is. I cannot imagine the amount of fae impressions he's mastered.

"But then, I caught wind of a shallow Sidhe fourth prince, who wished to prevent his siblings from reproducing, so that only he may have heirs to fill the throne. And do you know what he did?" He raises an eyebrow as if I don't know. "He used a particular set of witch sisters who specialize in halting heats. Since fae children are rare, and celebrated, this oddity would only be used on an enemy... or to help a *useless Unseelie* who wishes to continue being useless."

I wish I had been useless. "Useless? I did things for you that no one else could have done. You said so yourself." And the regret is visceral.

He steps closer, gripping my shirt when I try to back away. "That was then. What have you done for me this decade, pet? Nothing." He signals around my lavish room of teal fabrics and teak furniture. "You've lived like a princess when you deserved death. I gave you this life as a wedding present."

That's a lie.

He placed me in this castle as a spy so I'd be out of the way as he ruled the dark ones—the riffraff and chaos-makers who wish to burn down the fae world. Though I dare not say that aloud because I'm not sure of his, or his minions, actual intentions, and I'm not getting dragged into the pain of the liar's curse for this creature.

Leaning an elbow on my dresser, I attempt to appear calm. "I wouldn't deserve death had it not been for you. I'd never have..." I trail off because it feels dangerous to even mention the past here in the castle. By law and ethics, I deserve death. There's nothing honorable or right about what I helped with, even if I wasn't aware of the danger until it was too late. I should have seen him for what he was. Should have known better.

He shrugs. "You saved so many."

I lean close, positive my eyes are as red as the blood I helped spill. "Monsters. I saved monsters who didn't deserve saving."

The fake gray of Bogen's eyes slides into dark green with orange streaks and when he speaks, it is not a gentle, whimsical breeze. It's a growly rasp that promises torture, and I welcome it over the pretty mask of a fae I thought I loved. "And you're our useless Unseelie *pet*. You're done here."

My throat constricts, making my, "What?" come out as an embarrassing squeak.

He lifts his hand to wiggle my bespelled hair charm, jerk back when I make a grab for it. "There's an event approaching that will affect all fae. You will be with me when it occurs and then, maybe, you won't be so useless."

I know he wants a child from me. He believes my unusual lack of magic, and the power my father held, will double the mystical power of any child I bear. Just like it did for Bogen. It's possible we'd create the most magical fae in the world—one that may as well be a god that

Bogen will have control over, or so he believes. Not happening. He's too strong already. He's unstoppable as is. I shrug as if I could care less. "What's the event?"

"That inquisitiveness will harm you when we're home, pet."

His disgusting lair will never, ever be my home. "I'm better here. Remember? I give you information to keep your people safe."

"You think you're my only spy?" He grins. "You have one night. Pack your things and eat your last Unseelie meal. Tomorrow morning, you leave a note saying you've failed at freeing the missing king, and are traveling to seek council from other sources. The court will understand, and will soon forget you, or consider you lost when you don't return."

Air constricts in my lungs. I swallow, trying to loosen the tension. "It's not enough time."

"Oh, it is, though. Because of your little trick, I'm keeping you close. Before I had them killed, the witches confessed that since we're bonded, when your charm is destroyed, you'll only need to be near me to go into heat quickly. Perfect because..." He holds up a finger against the glamour's lips. "Well, pets don't need details, now do they? They only need to behave."

My mind races for a solution. I need to find another witch or warlock and have them cast another charm. It will probably cost me my wings or something equally important, but I need more time to figure out how to end Bogen. "Give me a week. I will come willingly, then."

"One night. And if you fail to show at the entrance to the Dark Forest by sunrise, I will find you in dreams and torture your lovers over and over again for our enjoyment. Show up, and I'll make things easy for you."

CHAPTER FIVE

DUCKS AND CLEAVAGE BALL

DONOVAN

Dinner in the castle isn't nearly as exciting when a certain Unseelie is missing.

I still can't figure out why Auralia acted like she did earlier—or odder than she usually acts around me. The strangers in the castle were merely visiting diplomarians. She didn't even show up to talk business with them, and she loves talking business. She wouldn't answer her bedroom door, and even though I could get in—locked or not—I didn't because I'm nice like that. Though, I thought about it.

I fold my cloth napkin from bottom to top and tuck in the sides as I stare at the open doors of the dining hall.

Our castle family, from cleaning crew to elders, line the tables, eating and catching up from the day—talking about weather and animals, new recipes, daily life, and gossip.

I usually love this time, but the words are mumbles and gossip doesn't stick in my head. Where is she? I slam my completed napkin sculpture on the table.

Jinora jumps beside me, and blinks her widened green eyes as she looks over my creation. "Is that a... duck?"

"It's a dove." I glance at the fabric's messy lines and crinkle my nose. "Or a duck. Whatever."

Jinora's hand alights on my thigh, and I want to fly across the room. She's my friend and nothing more, but days ago, she returned from a mapping excursion to the perimeter of the Dark Forest, and now she's been flirting with me publicly. Not in private. There, we're still as chaste as chatty siblings, catching up on gossip.

I don't know what her game is, but I don't like that she's been snappy when Auralia comes up in conversation.

"It's... charming." Jinora's thumb swipes against the cloth covering my thigh, sending my skin cringing.

Odd, because it's not like I don't enjoy fucking others besides—or especially with—Auralia. But a cycle ago, after too much wine, Jinora confessed she's a virgin and will stay that way until she bonds. It's an unusual thing for an Unseelie to do—we run hot and open with our sexual relations. At least most of us do. There are some non-court rebels who have their own ways.

I move my leg. I don't want to bond with Jinora.

"Donovan?" Jinora's gaze is soft and sweet.

Reluctantly pulling my attention from the door, I scoot my chair back and away from her. "Yeah?"

"You're distracted and..." Her eyes flit to the doors. "Oh."

Auralia stands in the room's entrance, eyes locked on mine.

All the sounds disappear, leaving us staring at one another in this rare void we seem to always have.

There's a touch to my face.

I jerk back with a vicious hiss before, realizing it's just Jinora. Breathing out, I wince at her shocked expression. *Whoops.* I squeeze her hand and press it to my chest. When I glance past the noisy crowd toward the doors, Auralia's gone. I shoot to my feet and spot her, taking a seat next to Ember, who feeds her a fried clover petal.

Typically, Auralia sends me warning glares to steer clear, until I catch her eyeing me with heat, amusement, or jealousy. That's when her sharp guard lowers enough for me to get close to her. However, tonight she's staring at the crowd with a slight frown that disappears when someone asks her something. Then it's fake smiles and fluttering lashes and looking anywhere but in my direction.

"Donovan?" Jinora growls, and jerks at my hand to make me sit down. "She's not good for you. You need to let that go."

"Do I?" I settle back in my seat and wave at a group of younglings, staring at me with confusion. I'm still riled up from Auralia's and my earlier encounter, and that clearly shows. "I don't think I want to." Picking off a chunk of cacao bread, I roll it into a ball, then launch it at Elder Bramblin's remarkable cleavage. It lands perfectly in the chasm and the group, who was staring at Jinora and me, cheer loudly enough to pull the attention of the room. Elder Bramblin's giggle sounds over the laughter as her mate, Linora, licks between her mounds to get the treat.

Shoving a chunk of bread in my mouth, I lean back with a smile. Auralia keeps her eyes on her plate and talks with Ember.

"Does she look sad?" I whisper. "She looks sad."

Jinora sighs. "Want to fly tonight?"

I should. It would get me out of this castle and away from Auralia. I want her to explain what earlier was all about, but she's avoiding my gaze, making it clear she's not interested in sharing. I don't need to wait around for an answer that's not coming. So I stand, gather our empty plates and offer a hand to Jinora. "Sure. Let's go fly."

She beams up at me, slipping her fingers into mine.

CHAPTER SIX

THE START OF GOODBYE

AURALIA

I pace outside Donovan's room.

He's probably not even in there because he's with Jinora, holding her damn hand, or far, far more. I'm caving in.

How could Bogen think one night would be enough?

I should have just gone with my horrible husband. What's the point of drawing this out?

Still, my feet refuse to take me away from this door. I lean closer and inhale.

Donovan's scent lingers, lessening the anxiety in my chest, though it shouldn't.

I'm gone soon. How long will it take my room to smell like castle walls when I'm no longer here? A few days? A full moon cycle?

The door opens, making me jump.

Donovan grips the frame above his head with a thickly toned, bare arm. He's only in low-slung pants and his hair's damp. "Are you pacing outside my door for a reason, Aura?"

I glance past him to his empty bed. It's not in shambles, like we make it when we're together, so they weren't in here at least. I want to run my finger over every faint scar and indent of muscle on his torso. "Am I keeping you from... something?"

The corner of his lips quirks up. "No. I just returned from a flight with Jinora."

This is a cruel farewell. Donovan and I have never flown together. That was my doing, as I feared one of Bogen's many spies would see us and get the wrong idea. Looks like Donovan and Jinora will be just fine once I'm gone.

"Good for you." I twirl a lock of my hair around my finger and tug it tight. "I wrote a letter to the nymphs about Kage. It won't go anywhere, but I thought you should know—"

Donovan takes my wrist and drags me into his room, shutting the door, and pressing me against it. His closeness calls to every inch of me. "Why are you really here, Aura?"

To say goodbye. To get a final taste of his lips and fill my nose with his scent, so I'll have one last good memory before I enter the hell I always knew was coming.

"Why do you think I'm here?" Dropping to my knees, I tug at Donovan's pants with my free hand, since he's still holding my wrist.

His pierced cock bobs free, and while I'd usually just suck him until he whimpers, I trace the vein on the right and tap my thumb over each of his four piercings, continuing down through his coarse hair, until I cup his balls. I explore how they tighten with my light touch.

His low growl is a sound I'll miss.

I grip the hard length of him, stroking my thumb up the underside of his shaft. This cock is perfect.

"I didn't fuck her." His words pull me from my dick enchantment. "What?"

He runs his knuckles down my cheek, sending sparks over my skin. Thankfully, before I can moan or lean into him because of his sweet touch, his fingers wrap around my throat. "I didn't fuck her, so lose the hesitation and suck my cock."

The relief is immediate. For tonight, he's mine, and I need him to push me through this. If he clears my head of everything but lust, I won't do something stupid like tell him every secret I've kept from him or confess that he means more to me than he could have ever guessed. It has been so exhausting doing what I need to, but not what I want.

I lift my chin. "Make me."

Red tints his deep brown eyes and his lips part, showing off the points of his fangs. He drags me closer by my throat. "Open." His voice is a dangerous grumble, though he's not dangerous to me...well, physically.

I lick my lips and refuse, because this is our game—our normal. We taunt, tease, and finally relent. Our power play has been the highlight of my existence and it's nothing like the few nights I had with Bogen in his disguise. I can lose myself in Donovan. Forget everything, though not for long. I squirm, but his hold is tight on my throat.

He presses the hard head of his cock to my closed lip and reaches into the top of my loose shirt to pinch my nipple.

I cry out, and he pushes himself into my mouth.

"Good girl," he says with a smirk.

Well played. Wrapping my lips around him, I suck and explore his piercings with my tongue.

His fingers slowly release my neck, then trail through my hair as he groans what nearly sounds like a purr. "Deeper."

Clawing at his hips, I take him down as far as I can.

He curses, rocking his hips like he can't help himself and when our eyes meet, an electric snap zings through me.

I'm going to miss him so much. Emotion tightens my throat, and I gag until I cough, then pull away. "I should go."

His chuckle is dark. "But we both know you won't."

CHAPTER SEVEN

THIS IS WHAT WE'RE MADE OF

DONOVAN

Renewed energy floods through me as if Auralia breathed it into me through my cock. Avoiding Jinora's airborne attempts to get close to me left me tired, but how can I be exhausted anywhere near Auralia?

She wipes spit from her chin with the back of her hand. Her eyes are watery, and if I didn't know her better, nor just had my cock in her throat, I'd think she was upset. But Auralia doesn't get upset—anger she does exquisitely, and nonchalance is her resting face. However, tonight, on her knees, she seems a bit lost. I guess she needs me to lead, which I'm more than happy to do.

"Up." I grab her arm and tug her to her feet. "Strip." When she eyes the doorknob, I press my hand against the wood and lean close enough to rub my nose against hers, but I don't, because she wouldn't allow that sort of affection. "Do you want to leave?"

"No." There's the anger. She pushes me back and jerks down her leggings, kicking them and her slippers off like they did her wrong. Her shirt is next, and it thwacks me in the face. Just as it drops, her lips crash into mine and she wraps me in her arms, holding on with a trembling tightness. *My jealous female.* She's never wanted to fly with me, though. I should press that more. Maybe in a couple days, when we're not sore—because we're going to be sore—I'll ask again.

I lick her tongue and nip her plump bottom lip, spinning us and walking her backward toward the bed.

She shoves down my pants the rest of the way, climbs me, grips and directs my dick to press against her wet heat.

When we fall on the bed, I slip into her hot pussy and nearly die. There is nothing better than being inside her, close to her. It's universe expanding.

"Fuck, I love this pussy." The words just slip out. They have before as well, and then she left me with a hard, wet dick and I didn't get her back in my bed for too many moons. I gather her hands above her head and thrust hard. If I distract her, she'll forget... probably.

She struggles and I grimace, pulling away, sure I've lost her for tonight, but her legs hold my hips tight to her, and it seems that her struggles are to get closer. "Please, Donovan." Her eyes are pleading. "Don't go."

What in the starry sky is this game?

Under me, she writhes on my dick, though I'm not moving. This is going to take testing.

I kiss her hard nipple, then give a gentle peck to the other.

She doesn't have one snarky thing to say? Not a, "get on with it," or, "stop trying to be sweet and fuck me already?"

When I graze my fangs over her neck like a mate would, she arches, giving me full access instead of knocking my face away with her chin. I stare into her red eyes and give her lips the gentlest peck; one she'd never allow me to give her without a hiss of warning.

The moan she exhales may as well be a shot of wormwood liquor with how I melt against her to consume her sweet mouth.I let go of her wrists.

She cups my face, and I'm pretty sure I've slipped into an alternate realm where my best dreams are reality. I'll take it. And her. I'd take her any way she'd be willing to give me, but this, I like a lot.

I grip her thigh and press in deep.

She cries a pleasured note that sends tingles up my spine.

"Close already?"

"Keep going," she whispers. "Don't stop."

This isn't us. It's terrifyingly different and gives me ideas that we could do this—for good and forever. She belongs in my bed and in my arms. Maybe now is the time. Maybe I need more testing.

"I won't stop." I kiss her again, because she's letting me. "And I never want to, pet."

The unpleasant result is instant. She freezes up and tries to inch away from me backwards, separating our bodies. "I can't... this wasn't a good idea."

"Sorry. Stay." I drag her back to me and shush against her lips. "Stay, Aura." I hold her face and nip her until she's arching toward me, helping me push back between her legs, making us both moan. From there, I touch her with my usual desperation and keep my thoughts about us to myself.

She's not ready for us yet. I just need to wait a little longer.

Chapter Eight

LAST WORDS

AURALIA

I slide my finger down Donovan's straight nose as he sleeps. It's so hard to leave. I don't regret the night though. I've wanted to let him wrap me in his charming warmth for so long.

And he did. At least at first.

Then we did our usual—hard fucking while taunting each other, though with a newfound sweetness that sent a different ache through me. *Heartbreak.*

I've felt it before. This time, it's more difficult in some ways and easier in others. I knew saying goodbye was coming at some point, so I was prepared, but this isn't betrayal or fury, just pure loss of something I want so badly.

Careful not to wake him, I inch closer. Each movement sends a twinge through my center, and I'm soaked from us both. I'm tempted to meet Bogen smelling like the best sex of my existence, hair a mess, and full of Donovan's seed, but he could lash out. He knows Donovan and I are lovers, though I'm lovers with many, so I'm hoping that keeps us both safe. Bogen can't view my feelings as long as he doesn't read them on my face, but if I sleep, he can find me, and I won't lead him to Donovan. Which is why it's time to say goodbye and keep this night locked in my memories.

My throat is tight as I inhale Donovan's neck. My mouth waters to bite him, which is ridiculous since I'm mated, but maybe my hatred for Bogen has morphed the bond into something different—something that would like to complicate the magic. Or maybe my body is as upset to leave Donovan as my mind is and is seeking a deeper physical connection to him, even if it wouldn't be real. I'm going to miss everyone, but, he, I'll miss the most.

"I wish I belonged to you, my love," I whisper across his skin and into the silence. "Sleep well." I take one more second of his warmth and scent and energy, then I dress, and sneak away.

The castle is quiet; though it's always quiet in the royal wing as there are so few of us stationed here.

My mother was a princess of a court so minor, the Enforcer Court absorbed it when she was wedded to my father. He is an elder full of magic, and will not acknowledge me as his own because of my lack thereof. Or maybe he didn't want to care for me after my mother's death when I was too young to remember her. Either way, I only live in this wing because of treason and pity. Or I *lived* in this wing. That's over now.

I bathe quickly, trying not to let the hurt sink too deep when geranium soap replaces Donovan's scent, then take my bag, kiss my bedroom door, and sneak into the king's office to write the letter Bogen demands of me. I have to be brief on details, but directly tell Typhon not to drag me back to the castle with his powers.

The prince can pull what he wants through the earth—an incredibly powerful magic, but it won't work through some wards and types of ground like glaciers or volcanos. He tried to bring Kage back to our court when we realized he wasn't returning, but received a shock from the nymphs' hexed ward that knocked him senseless for a couple of days, and we think his brother experienced the same magic.

I'm positive Bogen has wards in place where I'm headed. That could do a lot of damage, and we're already missing one king. We need Typhon, and are all so fond of him. I need to cut ties—should have cut ties with everyone I care about long ago.

I just hope my words are enough to keep my friends away. They can't get involved in this. If there's a silver lining, it's that I'm flying away from here with no more bloodshed. I open the king's office window and step onto the balcony, quietly closing the glass doors.

The patrolling guardians are nowhere in sight, though our wards are strong, so it's not always necessary for them to lose sleep when enemies can't get in.

My throat tightens as I leap for the sky, staying close to the canopy of trees, letting the wind dry my eyes. As I fly, the sky lightens to pink and teal, giving me a warning to speed up, but when the edge of the Dark Forest comes into view, my situation becomes so real that I have to land on a tree and cling to leaves, trying to ground myself from the panic flooding through me. This is it. My life will now be under lock and key.

Bogen will try to touch me again, except this time, I'm fully aware of the monster he is.

When sun warms my wings, my nose tingles from hyperventilation and my fingers ache, knuckles white. I'll find a way out of this. The decade of reprieve from my husband had my guard down, but I have ideas I've collected through the rotations—I'm resourceful. I only need enough time to figure out how to fight with no magic and break the bond that doesn't allow me to harm him. I pull myself together as well as possible and fly toward the darkened path. A chill runs down my spine when I see a shadow.

The creature looks as if a toad was stretched, then folded into a fae shape and put into ragged trousers. He blinks goggled lime green eyes. Deep folds act as cheeks that surround a wide hooked nose with bulbous flared nostrils. "You're late." His voice is like two bumpy stones grinding together.

I walk past him, toward the narrowing trees. "But I'm here." The last place I want to be. "Show me to my room, Bogen. I have a lot of sleep to catch up on."

"Not for long." He bares his knobby teeth at me and pulls my bespelled hair from his pocket as well as a flint spark starter. It takes one click to catch the hair and before I can grab it and fly, it's in flames. Guess those leaves were extra crispy after ten rotations. As chunks of sizzling ash drift to the ground, Bogen shoves me toward a narrow patch of trees with a grubby four-fingered hand. "There."

The portal is a dark shadow against an old palm tree. Another push from him sends me through and into a dark cave with two massive, golden doors tucked in the stone.

I don't pass the ward in place, but I can feel it tingling close by. As soon as Bogen steps beside me, I shove him against a stalagmite, sending him into a fit of growls.

I tilt my head. How deep does our bond go? A push is nothing, but now I'm regretting not bringing my mother's dagger. "Just testing our bond, since we vowed not to harm each other and you seem to love pushing me around."

"You harmed?"

My laugh echoes through the long corridor. "You have no idea."

And whether or not I go into heat, I plan to repay the pain he's caused the Unseelie court I love, and make his life as hellish as he's made mine.

Chapter Nine

WAKING UP IS HARD TO DO

DONOVAN

Daylight has never been my friend, but when it beams into my eyes, I snarl and search the bed with one hand for my female. Who is—I groan as I sit up and squint with one eye—Gone. *Fuck.* I meld back into the bed, inhaling the remnants of Auralia's scent. She always leaves, though usually just as I'm settling in for a decent snuggle.

Last night was different. We were together, I thought. Same page, synched orgasms, and a connection that splayed open my heart for her taking. It's hers. Yet, she didn't stick around. As usual. I had the sweetest dream about her, too. She was whispering something about her being mine and the thought tingles in my chest, making me grow warm.

We made a lot of strides last night, and I think things will be different between us now. They have to be, because I can't go backwards after a night like that.

My stomach growls, and then I growl and crawl out of the bed.

Auralia's clothes are off the floor. Maybe she went for breakfast. Or she's hiding away because last night was a lot. I stretch the soreness from my muscles, ready myself for breakfast, and walk to her door. When I knock, it's not Auralia who answers, but Ember.

I grin. "If I knew you'd be playing with Auralia this morning, I'd have woken up earlier."

"Donovan." Her voice is careful and downtrodden. It makes fear pop up and nightmare scenarios play through my mind.

"Is she okay?" I push the door open to find Jinora sitting on the bed, arms crossed and looking foul.

Typhon rummages through the dresser.

That doesn't help my panic. "What happened?"

Typhon slams a drawer and glances at me with a pained resolve that makes my hungry stomach drop. He pulls a paper from his pocket, crossing the room to hand it to me. "See what you can make of this."

I glance at Jinora.

She frowns at her lacy skirt, ignoring me.

I unfold the paper and lean against the wall as I read Auralia's short, to-the-point words—she's gone to gather intel that may help with Kage's imprisonment. She's not going into Rioch, but don't contact her or try to pull her back because it could be a danger.

Shaking my head, I study the atypically sharp angles of her signature. "I don't even know if she wrote this. She wouldn't leave." Not after that unless... I swallow hard. Unless she was saying goodbye. But that doesn't make any sense. Why would she be with me *like that* if she were leaving? Was it to lead me on, or so I'd miss her? I don't believe she'd do that to me. We have our fights, but under that is respect and far more than our teasing games.

"You okay?" Ember says, putting a hand on my forearm.

"This doesn't feel right." I shake my head and press my fingers into my tired eyes. "I don't know why she would leave."

Typhon approaches with a sigh. "She's never been completely comfortable here and when Kage was detained—she's taken a lot onto herself. Maybe she just needed a break to think and find a solution to get him back."

"She doesn't do breaks," I growl, voice low and warning. "And she's always thinking."

Typhon drags Ember behind him and steps back. Jinora now has her assessing eyes on me.

I let a little more of the inner fire rumble out because if I cork it, I may lose complete control. "Why are you here?" I ask Jinora. "In Aura's room."

Jinora's lips part, but she bites the bottom one and looks away.

Typhon speaks up and tells me about Auralia's note calling out Jinora's bruise.

When I step closer to my friend, she rolls back with surprising quickness, putting the bed in between us.

I glare. "Why are you nervous?"

"Because you look like you are going to tear apart anyone who gets near you."

"I won't. Are you hurt?"

She remains silent.

My fangs descend. "Who hurt you?"

Her eyebrows angle into a sad, please-don't-make-me-say-it expression. Fae are good at hiding truths, but stress slips out in our expression sometimes when we're at our wit's end with the liar's curse, and someone is treading too closely to a secret. "I'm not telling you."

Something is very off. It's beyond a coincidence that Aura leaves on the same day that Jinora is injured but won't talk about it. "You will though."

CHAPTER TEN

FOUND OUT SOMETHING INTERESTING

DONOVAN

Every day that Jinora remains silent and Auralia remains gone, grates at my nerves. I'm sour and our people know it and most likely know why.

For a week, I sleep in fitful patterns despite being exhausted from flying around the territories, talking to anyone who may know which direction Auralia went. None of them do. It's like she poofed out of existence.

Then, on the ninth sunset after she left, I find something that makes my edginess nearly consume me. I return to the castle, and meet with Typhon and Ember, who order additional guardians for Jinora's room.

Before we turn down her hallway, Typhon squeezes my shoulder. "Are you fine to do this? I can handle it if it's too..." His brows furrow. "Overwhelming."

He nailed that.

I am overwhelmed with anger and worry about what really happened to Auralia and what the information I found out could mean. I shake my head though, because I have to be in that room so Jinora can explain to my face what is going on. "Jinora's silent time is done. She's involved, and I need to know how." I squeeze Ember's hand and head down the hall.

She's worried too, but both Typhon and Ember have been checking in to the point of spoiling me. They've been involved in a lot of Auralia and my bedroom antics and can guess how I feel about her.

And now, I'm wishing I'd given Auralia more of my thoughts, and maybe in return she would have given me more of hers. Even if we fought about it or it wrecked us for longer than a couple couple moon cycles. She might have run, but she did that anyway.

I knock and step into Jinora's room, which is decorated to be just as bright and frilly as she is.

"Hello." She appears calmer than I believe she is as she sits in a pod chair at her small table, swirling a spoon in a cup of nectar. "I've missed you."

"You've seen me every day."

"You could see me more, you know." The intention is obvious and pisses me off.

I sit in the chair across from her. "This discussion again? I'm not letting Auralia go, and you know it."

"She's not coming back." She scrunches her nose, then tames her expression in a flash, but I caught it. She made a mistake.

I tilt my head. "Why is she gone?" If Jinora hurt her, I will—

She shrugs a shoulder. "Because it's Auralia. Her parting was inevitable."

I tense, ready to spring, and give two stomps to tell Typhon, Ember, and the guardians stationed at every exit to be ready. "Is that right, Jinimadoras Regine Balorian?" Funny how dropping a fae's full, real name changes the power in a room.

For a split second her eyes widen, then she squeezes them closed and lets out a short huff. "Please don't make me leave."

That is not what I expected.

And it gets weirder when she turns a determined gaze on me, leaning closer. "Bond with me. Let me stay here and be your wife."

I tilt my head. "You're an assassin, Jin. One from the tribes on the outskirts of the Dark Forest. You've been infiltrating our court."

She shrugs. "And you're in love with someone who will never be yours. We all have our issues."

I huff a laugh at her audacity. "Where is she?"

"I won't." Jinora—Jinimadoras's—lips firm. "He will murder them."

I shake my head in exasperation. "I swear to fuck, Jin. What in the pantheon of Zeus is going on?"

"Speak an oath to marry me and let me stay. It's what he wants."

I furrow my brows. "Not in the seven realms. Speak."

She hisses, eyes going red, then stands and steps toward the window. "You may as well come in, Hales. Morti. Better than eavesdropping." Does she have an accent? She glances at the door. "You too, Prince and princess. Vemmi, you're such a heavy breather. Hales is going to take your place as gentry if you can't be more stealthy."

It's my turn to go wide-eyed. Do I truly know anyone in my life? I know Typhon. We sprouted wings together—can't fake that.

The crew wanders in through the door and windows, weapons in hand, and looking more than slightly angry.

Sparks light Ember's fingers as she clenches her fists. "Where's Auralia?"

Jinora stares her down with such force, I ready myself to leap between them. "If I tell you, he'll kill my siblings and torture me further. You don't know what he can do."

I slam my hand on the table, sending the nectar cup toppling, and stand. "Who?"

"Promise yourself to me and—"

I grip her throat and flap my wings, surging forward.

She has a dagger against my neck the moment her back hits the wall. Did she have that hidden in the frills of her dress?

"Do it," I growl, leaning into the blade and letting my claws press into her soft skin. "And who will protect your family? Will the one threatening you set them free when you're gone?"

"You'll protect them?" Her eyebrows furrow and she glances at the dagger against my neck as she thinks.

"If you tell us where she is," Ember says. "We'll do what we can to protect your siblings as long as the situation allows it."

"The *situation*." She laughs. "As long as me and my kin, if they're still alive, follows your every rule, you mean? Too late for that, princess."

I'm quickly losing patience. "At the moment, you're not with us. You're with whoever has you scared. You're supporting someone who has taken a valuable member of the Crown Unseelie Court."

"She went. He didn't take her." She drops her gaze when her words hit me like a boulder.

I drop my fingers from her neck, but stay against her dagger's edge. "We'll do this with or without your help. But, as is, you're a traitor. Only you can fix that."

Jinora's jaw works. "He will know it came from me."

"If we strike fast and hard, he won't have time to harm anyone." I let a bit of my magic slide over her blade and it bends away from me until it's a circle of metal. "Is he stronger than the Unseelie army?"

She hisses through her teeth. "I liked that weapon." She definitely has an Outland's accent she's been disguising. "I... don't know. No one truly does, except maybe Auralia."

Typhon takes a step forward. "You have our word that we will protect you and yours as well as we can if you help us. That's your option, or we announce to the realm who you are and that you're protecting information about Auralia's disappearance. I'm positive that will bring more attention than you'd like, yes?"

For a moment, I'm afraid she'll pull another dagger from somewhere and slit my throat, but she relaxes against the wall, stares up at the ceiling, and blows out a long breath. "Auralia is with the Bogeyman." That name sucks all the heat out of my limbs. But then she continues, sending my entire world into crackling ice. "Her husband."

Chapter Eleven

SECOND HONEYMOON

AURALIA

B ogen shoves himself through my door mid-evening, just as he does every day. He kicks at the chair I put in the direct path of entry to annoy him.

My jail is a tower chamber with one barred window facing a chasm that drops who knows how far down into the depths of this cave. It used to belong to the Sidhe, who called it Klellic Keep. Bogen and his dark ones took it over after the Unseelie annihilated the dark fae they thought were a threat.

Lying on the tattered cot, threadbare pillow wedged under my head, I don't look up from my book on Sidhe history. "So punctual, *husband.*" I use the word now as a slur that grates on his nerves, which is why I say it as often as possible.

Lumbering toward me, he leans over the bed to inhale against my neck. I roll my eyes. He wants what neither of us have control over. If anything, my reproductive bits have shriveled up just from being around him. Though, that could be from the recent dreams of sex and the memories of our bonding that I swear he's infusing into my mind, because I've never had a sex dream about him before. I don't like how that makes me feel—like the moment my mental guard is down, he gets to break me even more than he already has.

He growls. "Why aren't you in heat yet?"

I shrug. "No idea. Maybe I need more of those sweet fig bites that Hurna makes."

The young Brownie kin is the nicest being in this dreadful lair, and they can cook anything. I hate that they're caught up as well, indebted to Bogen, even if their presence makes me feel not so alone amongst the lair residents who are loyal to the powerful fae legend. There are many who are here by deception. Bogen should be worried I'm getting to know them, but he seems preoccupied with my potential heat.

"Feeding you sweets doesn't seem to be making you any less useless." He grumbles again and then steps back. "Maybe if I..."

Dread washes over me as I realize what he's going to do.

Gray-green limbs shrink and change shape, and his bulbous features become slender and defined. Within seconds he's beautiful. And panting. The shift seems to take a lot out of him. I don't remember noticing that before, though I was busy screaming, and could have missed it. Adding "difficult shift change" to my "Bogen's weaknesses" list.

I thrust my hands out as he lumbers closer in Unseelie form, but he grips my ankle, dragging me to him.

He pins me under him, and I want to throw up.

There is nothing fake about my gag, or the lurch my stomach makes.

He looks on in confusion. "This form no longer appeals to you?"

"No," I grumble, trying to back away from him, remembering my naivety of wanting Duke Cherune so much that when he approached after ignoring me our entire lives, I fell right into Bogen's trap. The monster had murdered Cherune and wore his appearance like a masquerade costume, and I'd thought he was everything I needed in life. I wish I would have grown up sooner. "Get away from me before I destroy the upholstery, and you have to call in your angry servant girl to clean it up."

"She's not my servant, *pet*." His floral scent—Cherune's scent—washes over me, churning my stomach more. Bogen lowers his face closer to mine as if he's about to kiss me. "Maybe if we mate, your body will be more accepting of its needs."

"That's not how it works. I'm repulsed by this form." I force myself to stay calm and nonchalant. "The witches were telling you whatever you wanted to hear. They could have been liars like you." It's been far longer than he was told it would take for me to go into heat.

"You did something. You have another relic."

"Fresh out, so unfortunately." I twist out of his grip and unfurl my wings to glide across the room, but the gashes Bogen had his followers put in them haven't healed yet and air uselessly floats through the slowly closing gaps.

The scent of wine and cacao flashes through my senses and I stumble, sliding to my knees before pushing myself up and turning to Bogen, crossing my arms to hide my pebbling nipples. That reaction has to be because he mentioned my lovers, and Donovan came to mind. The phantom scent of him is just my hope, somehow still hanging on. But the last thing I need is for Bogen to think my body's response is for him.

I glare. "Or maybe we're not as bonded as we think we are." This is dangerous territory, and will cost me in nightmares that will stick with me for eternity, but I need to know more. Things aren't adding up like they should.

In a true bond, Bogen and I shouldn't be able to hurt each other or revel in our mate's pain like he did when his not-a-servant stabbed my wings. I'd also feel affection and a draw to him like I did when we first met. I wanted him so badly. Even after he showed me his real face, I felt the need to be near him.

Now I feel nothing but disdain and regret toward him, even when waking up from dreams where I acted the role of his mate.

I just want to go home, and spend another night with Donovan, plan Kage's escape, and get back to normal. I can't seem to let go of those hopes, or this itchy ache in my chest.

He raises a sculpted eyebrow. "Our bond is intact. Perhaps I'll remind you again when you sleep tonight." He grins when I can't hold back my wince. "You remember, don't you, pet? How warm you felt and all the words you said."

I grin, showing fangs. "I do, and I wish I didn't. You can leave now, Bogen. I'm not in heat, so take your small, limp dick, and shoo. I'm sure I'll see you tomorrow."

He glares and storms to the door, pausing to glare at me and bare his straight Unseelie teeth before slamming the door.

I let out a long breath and rub my forehead. I need a better game-plan. More—

There's a clank of metal, a whoosh of wings, and a hand covers my mouth, which I bite.

My attacker lets me go with a quiet hiss, and when I spin to confront them, heat swirls in my chest.

Chapter Twelve

Hello Again

DONOVAN

"Ow," I whisper-yell, glancing at the bleeding wound on my palm. Putting my attention back on my Auralia, I grin. "Only you would tell your abductor that he has a small, limp dick. Wait, have you seen—nevermind don't answer that." I grip her neck with my uninjured hand and pull her until I have her lips against mine. And, even here, in the depths of Klellic Keep, a place where the legendary Bogeyman is hiding, everything is right again. I wrap her in my wings, pulling her body flush with mine as she opens to me with a moan.

Yes, love. But not here.

I back us toward the window. Fortunately, I was able to bend a big enough gap between the bars. I didn't even have to squeeze through. Why the Sidhe needed a massive window to overlook a dark pit is beyond me.

Auralia gasps and pulls back, so I kiss her chin and neck, too thrilled to have her in my arms again to stop swooning all over her. "Wait, Donovan. How did you even get here?"

"Because I'm the best at hide and seek. But the better question is, 'how will we get out?' to which I will say, 'like this.'" I fall backwards out the window, taking Auralia with me.

The cavern is deep and dark and has a small cave entrance I doubt anyone has noticed, since it's not warded.

Auralia gasps and fights.

I let her go with a laugh so she can fly.

"My wings," she screeches as she plummets.

My grin falls away as I realize she's extended but barely able to glide.

I dive, heart racing and body aching in full panic mode. The light dims and disappears and while I can see well in the dark it takes too long to adjust, so I'm left groping air as I flap straight down. There's not enough time. I press my fingertips to the Seelie amulet Ember let Typhon and I use so I could call to him when needed. It's needed.

"Donovan." Auralia's voice is weak with fear, and it makes a jolt hit my chest.

I tuck my wings as the rock walls close in, and finally touch her fingertips.

Our palms slide together and I grip and jerk her against me, unfolding my wings to catch the air as we get too close to the ground too fast, but Typhon was ready and the ground rumbles and dips, opening up and reaching for us.

I wrap my wings around Auralia and crush my eyes closed, hoping this works.

We enter the ground like it birthed us backwards and within seconds of hard magical travel through the earth, we're reborn in the castle's training field.

I stagger to my feet, pulling Auralia with me and checking her over.

When I get to her back, she tucks her wings tighter.

"Let me see," I grumble.

Her jaw stays tight, but she relaxes her wings.

When I tug on her outer bone, extending the membrane, my fangs drop hard and Ember gasps from behind me.

Auralia has four big gashes on that are not new, because they're healing. They clipped her damn wings.

"Open it back up," Auralia says, rushing past me to the indented spot. She looks at Typhon with wild eyes. "Open it, now. I have to go back."

"Yeah, open it." I step close, eyeing the ground. "I'm going to kill him."

Ember growls, stepping beside me. "Why do you want to go back, Aura? Your home is here."

There's a crack in Auralia's rageful expression.

I take that as an invitation to give up revenge for a moment, and move in. I circle her waist and pull her close. "You belong here." *With me.* "Not with him."

Her eyes widen, but she settles her palms on my chest. "What do you know?"

"That the Bogeyman is your..." I can't stop the snarl, and I'm positive I look like death come to life. "Husband."

She winces, but then raises her chin. "Then, you understand that I can't stay here."

"Yeah, you can. And will." I'll tie her up if I must.

She glares up at me in that way that makes my cock jump because it doesn't understand this is an important conversation, and not tackle-Auralia-time. Her eyes go soft, lips parting in a tiny, sexy gasp, so I'm sure she can feel the bulge of me against her lower stomach.

"Auralia," Typhon says, putting a hand on my shoulder, making me growl. His fingers fall away. "We need to know what we're dealing with and how this came about. We know enough but are missing a lot of explanation."

I lean in to nuzzle Auralia's neck. My mouth waters to nip her soft skin. She smells almost sweet, and I never want to let her go again.

Typhon clears his throat, but I ignore him as Auralia's fingers dig into my pectorals. "So the Bogeyman has many he's enslaved by force or manipulation. Can he really lie?"

Auralia nods and her breath catches as I trail my tongue over her collarbone. Fuck, she tastes good.

I missed her, but didn't even realize how much. I need to taste between her legs, lap at her pussy until she's screaming my name.

"He," she whispers. "He can do other things…" She moans when I graze my fangs just under her ear. "This is very distracting, Donovan."

"Good," I grumble. Let her forget that she's actually considering returning to him.

"He'll find me. Us, actually. When he realizes I'm gone and I sleep, it's over." She does a half-ass job of struggling before giving up and wrapping her arms around my neck and openly allowing my nuzzles as I wrap around her further. Her wings are so warm tucked over my arms. She pushes my face away with hers and looks up at me. "And it's not just that he'll find me; he'll create my worst nightmares over and over until I lose myself in them. Then, he'll take what he wants from me anyway."

"And what's that?"

Her eyes scrunch. "Who gave you information about him?"

"Jinora." I smirk at the fire that enters Auralia's gaze. My jealous female. "She's not who we thought she was."

"I need to speak with her, and then I have to go." She steps away from me.

I grip the back of her neck, and press my forehead to hers. "I will kill him before you get there."

Typhon gives an approving hum from behind me.

Auralia grips my shirt, balling it into her fists. "You can't kill him. No one can. He's impossibly strong, conniving, and can skin-shift into anyone he wants within seconds. You could try to fight him, and he'll turn into me. Would you murder me?"

Rage simmers in my spine, aching to be released. "Never."

"Exactly. You will hesitate. And it will be over. I don't want you near him and his army." I've watched Auralia long enough to recognize the firm set of her lips and worried angle of her eyebrows means there's something else she's not telling me, and she's about to bolt. It's almost like she's ashamed. Maybe it's because of her pride and how she got into the situation. She swallows and looks to the castle. "Where's Jinora?"

"The dungeon," Ember says.

CHAPTER THIRTEEN

OH, THAT'S NOT IDEAL

AURALIA

I don't want to let go of Donovan, but I do. The need to press back against him is instantaneous. His heat and scent make me want to fall onto my knees and taste him before he slides between my legs and fills the ache that's back with a vengeance. I shake that off though.

If Bogen finds me, he knows how to punish me. He'll torture me in dreams and spill the secret he's held for a decade to the entire fae realm. When I do get away from him, I won't be able to return to any Unseelie court ever again. They'd kill me on sight.

Turning, I walk toward the castle, trying to adjust to the ache and swell between my legs.

Donovan grumbles and follows, stalking behind me like a predator, which does not help the excitement spiraling through my body.

I shove open the doors and take two steps in before Ember flutters up beside me, taking my hand.

"What's going on, Aura?" she whispers. "Really."

I shouldn't say anything, but it's not like I can get back to Bogen without their help. He clipped my wings—ironically to keep me there and now I can't return without days of travel.

I have no idea what to do, but have always understood this day was a possibility. It was the risk I took when I walked into the Crown Unseelie Court right after Bogen showed me his true form and I didn't confess or walk right back out. I got caught up by being afraid of my new husband and fearful of what had transpired because of my help. And now I can't keep these fae I've grown to love entirely away. If I attempt to escape now, Donovan will follow because he's determined like that. He needs to know things. It's why he's so good at being Typhon's second.

As if he heard my thoughts, Donovan growls from behind me. I glare at him over my shoulder, and his lips quirk, the charming dolt.

The guardians at the front doors nod at me, but look confused. Yes, I should be flying. When I turn toward the stairwell to the lower levels, Ember takes my hand in hers, squeezing my fingers.

I quietly begin the story. "When I came of age, he pretended to be someone I was desperate to have, but my feelings had been unrequited our entire lives. Bogen can shift into anyone—sound like them, smell like them—it's nearly flawless." I take the hall leading to the lower stairs. "I'd felt honored when Duke Cherune finally put his attention on me. Obviously, I didn't know it was one of the darkest fae legends himself in disguise. Things went quickly from there, we were married and bonded, planned to move South to be near his family, though I'm fairly certain they don't exist and then..."

My chest squeezes with the stress of remembering the past I can't tell my friends.

My new husband told me of a particularly magical place near the Crown Court's territory that was in danger from the vicious Sidhe. They were infringing on the local fae's rights and his family would be in danger if they succeeded. But there was hope. Because of my father's standing in the Enforcer Court, and because the princes had also lost their mother young, giving me a similarity to his sons that would press on the king's empathy, I would be allowed to speak privately to the king, to explain the growing problem.

I told the king, asked for his help to protect the area and the creatures that lived there, and invited him to fly there with me. I lured him, protected only by one trusted guard, so we didn't create concern before there needed to be concern.

I didn't know that Bogen was the threat. I didn't realize the story I believed so thoroughly that I could relay it with no consequence from the liar's curse, was completely false. Not until it was too late and my new husband stood smiling before me, covered in royal blood.

The first thing he said after I stopped screaming was, "I've always wanted to kill a king."

Donovan's thick fingers entwine with mine and I'm jerked from the memory. He kisses my head as if it's the most natural thing to do.

And I let him.

I clear the emotion from my throat. "And then Bogen showed me his true form. He left me alone for a while, and now he wants me back. Permanently."

"But why is he doing this to you?" Ember says, gently. "You didn't answer."

"I don't want to think about it."

"It's the only way we can help you."

I don't deserve their help. I shake my head.

Donovan turns me to face him. "You are going to get used to talking to me, because I'm not going anywhere, Auralia. Enough hiding. Explain."

He wants to know the harshness of my situation? My stupidity and flaws? *Of course he does*. At least, once he knows, he won't follow me back to Bogen.

I twist from his grip. "Fine. Because he wants a child with me. I am uselessly unmagical, which is especially painful considering who my father is. I'll spawn a severely magical child... or so Bogen believes."

Donovan's irises flash into crimson pools and the hair stands up on the back of my neck.

It's not a bad feeling though. It calls to me with the most intense need—my eyes widen. I'm warm and tight and antsy and—it can't be. It's not possible? "Oh no."

"What?" Ember says, then looks at Donovan and rolls her eyes. "He won't hurt you; he's just been in a mood since you've been gone."

"I'm not afraid of him." Pivoting, I rush toward the dungeon. I need information right now. Time is running out. I sprint down the stairs and rush into the dungeon area.

It has four rooms with ward-guarded glass.

Jinora sits on the stone floor in the corner of one like a discarded doll, even though there's a chair, table, and even a restroom behind a heavy curtain. She looks haunted and annoyed. Far different from her bubbly, but meek, demeanor.

Her eyes dart to me and widen. "Why are you here?" She's up and across the room in a second, tilting her head like a bird about to strike a fish. "You're supposed to be with him. Did he let you go? What did you tell him?" That is a unique accent. Almost like the banshees of Balor.

"Who are you really?" I ask.

She looks at Donovan. "You found her?"

"Of course, I did," Donovan grumbles.

She places her palms against the glass, appearing so desperate for information—something I'm familiar with. "Where did you find her? Were my siblings there?"

Donovan steps closer to me. "Dark Forest—Klellic Keep—and not to my knowledge."

"Is that how he's holding you to him?" I ask. We all have our reasons—our mistakes. "Threatening your family?" I shift to ease the ache between my legs, but it doesn't help.

She purses her lips. "Since it's likely I already have an execution demand on me... yeah."

I can't really be mad that she's the spy who's been keeping Bogen informed of my lovers and court business, because I'm also at the castle under false pretenses. I'm the enemy. But this needs to stop, and the more information I get, the better.

"Tell me everything, quickly. I'm going into heat, and I need a plan." I glance at Donovan, who's looking at me with both shock and need.

I have no idea what in the celestial bodies I'm going to do.

CHAPTER FOURTEEN

SO MUCH MINE YOU'D BE SHOCKED AT THE MINENESS

DONOVAN

Auralia is going into heat. As in, ready to be holed away fucking me, because I'm hers and she's mine. Probably.

It's a little unsettling she's going into heat as I stole her from her... husband. That word sits raw in my mouth, and I didn't even speak it.

Either way, she'll stay in heat because she's mine, or will slide out of it because she needs more time to be mine. If she stays in, a child may or may not occur. It's a one out of fifty shot, because fae bodies are as fickle and mischievous as their minds. I'm in.

Though, she doesn't look like she is.

She's pale and worried as she talks with Jinora about how she met this Bogen.

I know the legend of the Bogeyman. I can't imagine a fae who doesn't. He's a named Boggart; old and powerful. He's said to start wars between the fae and hoard favors like stones in a riverbed. I never expected Auralia to be involved with someone so evil, but she clearly doesn't want to be. And I hate that I didn't know this about her.

"And you remember him killing your friends?" Auralia asks, hand against the glass.

Jinora's eyes fill with tears. "How could I forget that?"

Auralia's eyebrows scrunch, but she nods, turning toward the stairs. "Goodbye, Jinora."

"Hey," Jinora yells, voice rasped and tight with desperation. "Let me out, so I can find my siblings. They need me."

"Not a chance," Auralia says before I can. "You'll go back to Bogen and tell him everything."

"He'll find out anyway. You know how he is."

Auralia pauses on the stairs and turns back to face the cell. "I hope your family is safe. It will take time for him to get through the ward though, and I need to get a plan together." She continues up the stairs. "Are there guardians available to protect her? They especially need to be near her when she sleeps."

"Yes," I say. "How does that work?" While I'm unnerved by Auralia's obvious stress, I'm still mesmerized by every motion she makes as she walks—her swaying hips, the tight tuck of her wings, and way her disheveled curls still bounce and shine like they're doused in autumn light.

Her shoulders lift and drop with a sigh. "From what I've experienced, it starts with nightmares as he works his way into the mind. It can take a few days to pinpoint, but then he manifests close to the person. It's painful and exhausting for the dreamer. But I think it is for Bogen as well. It's a big magic push." She aims for the castle entrance.

At the open doors, I grab her hand, tugging her back until she's looking at me. "No one is staying in the south tower room." Since only mates and those closest to her will be able to scent any biological change in her, we don't need to be out of the keep, and Bogen can't fly, from what I understand. I can get her out quickly, and he'd have to descend a maze of seven stories just to get out the door to follow us.

"And?"

Ember sighs, flitting toward Typhon and a pack of guardians, no doubt to give them more instructions while Auralia and I argue as usual.

I tug her closer. My mouth waters to taste her. "And you're staying with me during your heat."

Auralia's eyes widen and she looks outside to the now non-existent hole we popped out of. "Donovan, I—"

"That better not be 'can't.'"

"It is though." But she steps closer to me and that electricity rolls over my skin, stronger than ever. "I'm... unable to without..." Her brows furrow as she seeks words that won't get her caught in the liar's curse. Because she knows she can—and wants to—stay with me. "Repercussions."

"Which we will deal with. Life is full of choices, Aura. Are you choosing him over me?"

"No." She bites her lips together like she didn't mean for the truth to burst out.

"Then what is it?"

"You're in danger, and worse..." She shakes her head, but I hold her chin until she relents. "You don't even know me. You don't know what I had to do. What I'm really like."

"Yes I do." I grumble a purr and lean in to smell her neck. The faintest scent of almonds makes my eyes roll back. "I know when you're scared, jealous, and when you find me so amusing, you can't help but fight hard against a smile. I know your past has been full of secrets, and you will tell me more when you're ready. But don't think I will sway from wanting you, and don't tell me you're leaving. There are a lot of things I'd do for you, but letting you go isn't one of them."

She clutches my shirt with a neediness I haven't seen from her. The almond scent blooms.

I taste right under her ear, dragging an exquisite groan from her. "Come on."

I glance at Typhon who looks up at me with a pleasured smile.

He knows what I've always felt for her, and what it could mean if her heat sticks around.

How deep and how many times would I need to come inside her to unwind the bond of another?

She reluctantly follows me.

We'll find out.

CHAPTER FIFTEEN

THE WORST IDEA OF ALL THE IDEAS

AURALIA

My frazzled mind chastises my aching body with every step as I follow Donovan. *You're thinking with your cunt. You need to run away from everything. Do this alone, like you always have. Run now before he finds out everything about you and hates you forever.*

But I don't run.

I helplessly let him lead me through the castle because as soon as he entwined our fingers, our palms fused together, and I think I'd die if they separated.

We're stopped a couple of times by nosy Unseelie and Donovan works his charm to avoid questions of where I've been, teetering on the edge of truth and making me look far better than I really am. It won't take long for everyone to find out, though. The guardians are good with secrets, but often their bedmates are not. Rumors spread, often out of concern, but sometimes out of malicious intent.

Since I'm friendly with pretty much everyone besides Jinora, I'm not sure how long it will take before Bogen finds out I'm here because of gossip—though he could have more spies. The Court would try to protect me, at least until they found out how I got here. Then, they'd hand me over.

As soon as we're up in the tower room, I expect him to be on me, teasing my skin and sending us into a frenzy of ripped clothing and messy sheets, if we make it to the bed at all, but he lets go of my hand and steps to the window overlooking the land to the east.

He puts his hands in his pockets. "I'm mad at you."

I tilt my head. "Why now?"

He closes the curtain and leans against the wall. "Because you didn't talk to me. I would have been there for you. You wouldn't have had to leave and face him on your own."

"I would have. I still do."

"Stubborn." He growls. "I would never have called you 'pet' had I known why you hated it." He holds up a hand as I open my mouth to protest. "Yeah, I heard him. It took everything in me to remain outside the window and not barge in, but I wasn't sure you wanted me there until you insulted him."

"I didn't want you there," I choke out. "You could have been killed."

He steps forward, gripping the back of my neck and battling my gaze with his intensity. "If I could get you out of this situation, I would have taken my last breath with a smile."

"Stop it." I shove at him. "I'm not worth that."

He holds on a moment longer before letting me go. "You don't understand what you're worth to me. How do you not know how much I care for you?"

He can't mean that after how I've acted since we've known each other—us using one another, and keeping our distance unless the need got too great. I shake my head. "Don't waste your love on me, Donovan. You don't know what I've done."

"Then fucking tell me."

That's enough conversation for today. I'm too hot and there's a persistent and distracting ache between my legs. This can't be. Bogen said the heat would come on fast, but it should have tapered off being away from him. Unless...

I step closer to Donovan and he steps against me, inhaling my neck.

His groan makes my core clench. "Your scent is intoxicating." He just means my normal smell, right?

I grip his shoulder and the shock of the touch is almost too much to bear. "Donovan?"

"You're going to ask how quickly I can get my pants off, aren't you? The answer is, very, very quickly."

A laugh escapes me.

He grins against my neck. "I missed you, Aura." He lifts up to stare down at me, stroking my cheek with his thumb. "I missed how you watch me when you think I don't notice, and how you barely hold back your rage when I mess up my hair and make you think another female's fingers have been in it."

My mouth drops open. "You did not."

He arches an eyebrow. "Oh, I did." He runs his hands down my back and slips his fingers under the band of my pants. "I've never been with Jinora. She's just a friend." His brows crinkle. "I think."

"You did that to make me jealous?" I don't know whether to toss him out the door or shred his pants. My body screams for the destruction of his garments.

He hums affirmation. "That always led to you being in my bed or joining our lovers with me."

"I need you," I whisper.

His fingers skim over my ass, then upper thighs. Heat sears through me like a pulse winding tighter. He kisses my raised chin, following my jawline to my ear. "Tell me your secrets, Auralia, and I'll give you everything you want."

I huff a laugh at his audacity, but he moves his hand out of my pants, and moves away from me instead of closer like he should. "We're going to play a little game. It's called *time to fess up to your mate.*"

CHAPTER SIXTEEN

VICIOUS UNSEELIE

DONOVAN

Auralia's eyes narrow as she wiggles out of her pants for me. "You're not my mate."

"No?" I step behind her and trail my extended fangs against her neck.

She arches with a purr—an invitation.

I kiss her pulse and grip her hips. "You don't ache for me to bury my cock and my fangs inside you? What else happens when you're in heat around your mate? I know you've studied it."

"I just want you." She rolls her ass against me so temptingly. "The heat could be remnants from being near Bogen before."

I hum. "And that's why it's getting stronger?"

Apparently she's too far gone for my sarcasm, and frowns back at me, but then freezes. Her brows furrow, and she tilts her head as her eyes go unfocused. "He can lie." Auralia's mind is an impressive thing, if not rather odd, when she's working something out.

"Okay." I spin her to face me and run my fingers over the flush just below her collarbones.

She slaps my hand away, just to tug off her shirt and throw it. "Bogen can lie." She steps against me, pulling my hand fully to her breast.

Walking her backward toward the bed, I plan my next move. I play with her dusky nipple and dip down to kiss the other, which is already hard and tempting. I don't really want her thinking about Bogen at the moment, but I do want her to realize there's more between us than just lust. I will help her fight him. Plus, I think her secrets revolve around him and I'm going to need that information. While sexual torture isn't the kindest of acts—I push her down on the bed and I turn my hand, slipping her nipple between my first and middle finger, stroking the tip with my thumb, making her moan—it's better than other methods, and I'll do what I feel is necessary to get answers and make her mine. "That is a powerful gift for a fae. How did he escape the curse?"

She grits her teeth and arches into my touch. "I don't know."

"How would he have lied to you?" Then her vague words snap together into a picture that fills me with rage. "You think he made you believe you were bonded to him?"

"He's made me believe a lot of things." Her eyes flutter closed. "He's a dreamweaver—every vision he implants is so real. I've felt terrible things I thought were the truth when I awoke, but they weren't. And I've been—" She sucks in a breath as I switch to her other tit and work that one. "Suspicious."

I need her words as much as I need her body right now. "Good. Suspicious is a good way to be when dealing with enemies."

She turns her face away when I lean to kiss her. Her conscience isn't clear yet, then.

I tap her cheek until she looks at me. "There was something else though, wasn't there?"

Sure enough, her thinking expression angles to one of shame and my chest clenches. It's bad. Whatever she's holding back from everyone is eating away at her soul.

I run my hands over her heated wing arches.

She stretches them out for me, settling her wings on the soft bed, showing those cuts that should have never happened.

I drop kisses and licks down her neck as she lifts her hips toward me. *So tempting, love. But not yet.* "What has you feeling guilty, Auralia?" I press her down onto the bed with a palm when she tries to flee from my question, then nudge open her legs with my knee. "Tell me…" Blowing over her hot wings makes her suck in a breath, which makes me even harder. "Tell me and I'll be good for you. I really want to be good for you, Aura."

"Donovan." She whimpers and shifts, but keeps quiet otherwise.

Bad guy, it is. I nibble at her ear. "Did he tie you up? Force you to give information or your body beyond manipulation and dreams?"

"No."

"Okay." I keep her pinned and glance around the room for rope. My gaze lands on the silky braided curtain's tie backs. That will do. I weave my magic, bending the rope and curtains toward me so I only need to stretch to snatch the cord. I drop onto her fully, my lips on hers, opening her to me with hard nudges of my tongue, while I try to focus on getting the cord how I need it. That is a hard task considering how sweet her mouth is. Seriously, her taste has gone from perfect to perfectly sweet—like Aura dipped in fig sauce. Fortunately, the rope is looped on both ends, so it doesn't take much brain power to push the cord through the end, making a slip lead.

Auralia grips my hair and I groan, but pull her up to a sitting position, yank her left hand back and guide it into the braided loop. A quick tug makes the rope tight.

"What are you doing?" She doesn't seem upset about it though. Just curious.

"What I must do to make things clearer for you." I smile, taking her other wrist and moving it behind her, slipping on the lead so her hands are tied behind her back, under her wings. "Tell me what you're so guilty about."

"No."

I give her a wicked smile and push her back on the bed, then crawl over her. "You know, I've heard that being in heat gives the most intense orgasms. And the most intense need for them. But it doesn't just stop there, does it?" I brush my lips against her gasp. "I read too, love." Her skin is heated under my fingers as I work my way up her thigh. "You need your mate's touch, which is spurred on by being around them. So tell me, do you still think there's no bond between us?" I take my hand from her, just at the junction of her sweet thighs, and move away from her.

"Donovan," she growls.

"Say it. Say you don't crave my touch." My grin goes wider at her frustrated silence, because I know there's an end to this. "I will pleasure you as often as you need for the rest of our lives if you stop holding back with me. That's my intention, Auralia. Step five of our courtship."

"We can't court." She lifts her hips to me, presenting her pussy for me to devour. "Please." The desperation in her voice is as sweet as her scent.

"Tell me what he has over you."

She growls and drops her hips, straining to get her hands free. "No."

"Okay then." I sigh and lunge to lick her nipple, then up her sternum. I suck her neck, making her cry out.

Her wings wrap around to pull me closer, but I brace myself instead of sinking against her and with her injuries, she's not as strong as usual.

I kiss her earlobe and lick up to the pointed tip before whispering in a growl. "When you've had enough, you will tell me what I want to know."

CHAPTER SEVENTEEN

IS DEATH BY SEX A THING? PROBABLY

AURALIA

Not fair. My life has never been fair, but now Donovan is set on torturing me?

If I didn't love him so much, I might kill him for this. But the thought sits cold and impossible in my stomach, making me even more curious. I'm a jaded being—battle-hardy from every misstep and deception I've had to trudge through—but I'm also logical and well read. These feelings and facts...

I might be on the verge of matehood with Donovan.

I'm not allowed to acknowledge the excitement and relief. It can't be real, and there's too much of my past in the way.

But my body burns for him. The thought of me or anyone harming him makes sharp rage harden my bones. He smells sweeter than usual and yeah; I want to taste him—his mouth, his cock, his blood. My mouth waters and my pussy clenches.

This is... terrible. I've had a decade to understand that I'm stuck in a bond with Bogen until one of us dies. I'm not mentally prepared to add another mate into this dangerous equation. Am I bonded to both of them? Did the magical bond with Bogen trickle away when I met Donovan? Or is this a dream Bogen has concocted and when I give in, the worst of things will happen to punish me for merely living in the same world as the Bogeyman?

Donovan runs his knuckles down my side. "I can feel your worry."

I bite back my laughter, but it bubbles out anyway. "This might be a dream."

His eyes go worried, and he tilts his head. "That's a fear?"

"Yes. Reality is never real when the Bogeyman is your husband."

His scowl goes soft. "Do you remember the hunt Ty hosted? The first one that Ember attended?"

I flick my eyebrows up. "You caught her."

Donovan's nostrils flare. "And you caught me. Then, we had the most delightful time while Ty watched until he couldn't take it anymore. I threw Ember at him and tackled you. Remember?"

My breath quickens. "Of course I do." That had been one of the best days between us. Ember's taste had been on my tongue when Donovan thrust down my throat, more passionately aggressive than he'd ever been with me. I lift my chin to take his lips.

He gives me a teasing peck and moves back. "Bogen wouldn't know what I said, would he?"

I shift in the bindings he's put on me. "Unless he had shifted into you or had a spy. A dryad or something."

Donovan growls, and it sends the most delicious warning through my body. "I will bend him until he snaps. No, Auralia. *I* proclaimed that you were mine." The crimson that had been waning in his eyes brightens again.

"You had meant for the chase."

"I had meant forever." He teases my nipple with the most delicate touch.

Considering his words and the truth he put behind them, along with how much my body needs him, makes my eyes sting.

This path we've taken isn't what anyone could call romantic. We've spit vitriol at each other, then fucked a moment later and every time he got close—too familiar—I pushed away and ran, terrified he'd get caught up in my troubles. But he's in them, anyway. The thrum of connection with him is strong and wants to be stronger. Fate is odd. Maybe if I'd let him in sooner... I can't consider that. But I can consider him. And once we're fully bonded—if that's even possible—I should be stronger, lack of magic or not. Maybe there's a chance of living through this?

Jerking at the binds he put on me, I try to push up to get closer. "Forgive me, Donovan."

"For what?" His eyes go redder and the skin around his eyes darkens in warning.

"For dragging you into this. And for not being able to be what we both need. I'm sure there's more, but—"

"You are exactly what we need, Aura. But you have to give me everything you've been hiding."

"You will hate me. Probably kill me before the others have the chance."

He grips my face and kisses me hard. "There is nothing," he growls against my lips. "Nothing that will make me hate you. And no one will harm you. Not ever again."

I wish I had the faith in his words that he does. But if we even have a sliver of a chance to be together after Bogen finds me, we can't go in with this secret still between us. And I'm mentally exhausted. I've been ill over this for so long that another moment in this heat with my mate so close—holding back is impossible to bear. So I swallow down the tight emotion and let the truth go. "I'm responsible for King Redrik's death."

CHAPTER EIGHTEEN

PAUSE

DONOVAN

I shake my head at Auralia's words.

The Dark Forest Sidhe murdered Typhon and Kage's father along with an honored guardian. The war we brought down upon them was short, and we left nothing but dust in our wake.

"That can't be true." I edge back from Auralia to get distance from her scent so I can think.

"I told you." Auralia's face scrunches in pain, and she turns on her side. "Undo the bindings so I can go back to my *husband.*"

My magic loosens the knot, and Auralia gives a sharp sob as she pulls her hands in front of her, rubbing her wrists.

She moves to get up.

I crawl back to her and pin her under me. "I need to know more. How are you responsible?"

She huffs a sarcastic note. "I pleaded for his help and led him directly into a trap. I would never have—I didn't know Bogen was my new husband. There's not a chance anyone will believe that."

"I believe it. You can't lie."

"But Bogen can. He'll have everyone against me instantly. Me just being in the castle, allowing the lie to go on this long is enough for you to execute me for treason, and that's not even including the war that occurred because of the king's death." She pushes at me, though the mouthwatering scent of almond amplifies, as does the red in her eyes and the darkness touching her cheeks and collarbones. "That's my confession, Donovan. I'm a traitor placed in the kingdom by the influence of my Boggart husband. Just kill me and be done with it. I don't think he can find you yet."

"Aura," I coo. "I couldn't if I tried."

She shoves at me, and a tear slides down her cheek.

I grip her chin and lick the wet trail away. "I need to know everything, so I can figure out how to help get my mate out of this situation. You were there?"

She stares up at me, lips parted. Then, she nods. "I was. Bogen sent me before King Redrik to plead for help for the mystical beings of the Dark Forest. He'd told me that the Sidhe were encroaching on the lands and picking off or recruiting the most magical residents, so that they could eventually take the castle, Unseelie, and my new husband's family."

"Even if the dark ones, Sidhe, Trow, and every Boggart in the realms bound together to fight us, they'd lose horribly."

"You don't know his power. Without him, sure, but I didn't realize that until years later."

The need to comfort her wars with the need to know the full story. I stroke her cheek. "What really happened in the forest?"

Her eyebrows scrunch into a sad expression. "King Redrik agreed to a quick trip to the outskirts of the Dark Forest to discuss the matter with my new husband—a duke. When they met, Bogen sliced the king's throat while his minions bombarded his guardian. It was over so fast. I didn't know he could lie until I stood beside him at the castle, still in shock, as he recounted a completely false view of what happened. And I said nothing out of fear."

"He'd told us that you barely escaped with your life and that he needed to go check on his family, and couldn't take you for fear of your life and mind."

She bares her fangs. "My mind is a wreck. I'm always on edge; always guilty. He probably wanted me here to torture me further."

"I've tortured you a few times too, love." Unknowing that some teasing pushed her in ways that were cruel, because I didn't know the situation. I aim to kiss her, but she evades.

"Stop taunting me and tell me how you really feel about this. I am responsible for the king's death. *Me*. And I've been here a decade—"

"Helping his first born adjust as the new king. Making us stronger. You climbed the ranks because you're trusted and intelligent."

"Because I'm deceptive and pitiful."

"Never say that again." This is going to be hard to navigate, now and when everyone else finds out, but it doesn't stop her from being my mate and this is when she needs me most. I stroke her cheek with my thumb and feel dumbstruck by the tint of her blush. "You were deceived and have been protecting yourself ever since. You don't have to do that anymore."

She blinks up at me. "You're not... you're not rejecting me?"

Moving back, I shuck my pants. "No. And you're not rejecting me." It's not a question, because we're no longer playing the run-away game. "But for now, we're pushing all this aside, because you need me and I need you. Later, we're going to tackle the problem head on." I grip under her knees, pulling her sweet cunt within my reach. "You're mine, Auralia. Not his."

When I lap at her and kiss her clit, she keens, sinking her fingers into my hair and soaking my tongue.

I smile, though that was a little shocking. "Already?"

Her hips twitch as the aftershocks of her orgasm flow through her. "Heat." She tugs at my hair. "I need more."

Growling, I suck a mark onto her hip. "What do you need?"

"You. I need you. Now."

"Because you're mine."

She bites her lip and nods.

This moment calls for patience and going through the stages of courtship with her in order like a good Unseelie. But everything that's happened—everything I've learned—I can't bring myself to be good. Auralia is mine, just as I am hers, and no one, not even the Bogeyman is going to stop that.

I flip her to her stomach, and she lifts her gorgeous ass, groaning when I grip her hips, line the head of my cock against her, and sink home with a pleasured hiss.

Her body is strung tight under mine, and her wings are hot against my chest.

Holding her tight, I kiss her neck. "I'm yours forever, Auralia Auberdine Farnic." I pierce her skin with my fangs and when she whimpers, I bite down hard into her muscle and groan at the taste of her sweet blood.

Auralia screams, then pants as she relaxes under me. I don't know if she can feel the slight shift of magic. It's possible that she may not ever feel the same tug I do, but I'll just have to work that much harder to show her she's mine. When I unlatch from her skin and lick the wound, she surprises me by turning in my arms.

Her face is intense and shadowed with possessive emotion as she kisses me. She drags me to the bed and straddles me, sinking down on my cock. Leaning over me, she kisses my throat. "Donovan Kimon Germanthia, I belong to you." She is less gentle with her bite, and I couldn't be more thrilled as I jerk and yell out at the sting, yet tilt my chin up to give her more room.

Bound. Mine.

When she releases her hold, I flip her under me and pound into her. We're not a gentle couple, not sweet or soothing, even in this moment. We've waited so long for this, we rush headlong into the bond like it needs to be cracked to be obtained.

My muscles strain as the slow rolling magic shifts and settles, and when I can barely hold on a moment longer, Auralia's legs tighten around me and she shreds the sheets with claws I haven't seen on her before. I chuckle as she bares her fangs in the most gloriously pained look of pleasure.

She pulses heat around my cock and I'm lost to her.

I come with a roar, forgetting anything in this universe that isn't my mate under me.

My *mate* is under me. Mine and mine alone.

When I've given her everything I have to give, I lick her wounded neck again, happy to feel the mark already starting to heal. "So sweet, mate." When she doesn't say anything, I move to look at her. "Did I hurt you?"

She looks shaken and stares at the ceiling, hand on her chest. "I've never felt this before."

"Felt what?"

"Magic."

CHAPTER NINETEEN

THE NEWNESS OF YOU

AURALIA

There's magic coursing through my uselessly unmagical body. Donovan's magic. It's like it transferred to me so that I know it's there—so I know he's mine.

"Magic," I repeat, unable to hide the awe. "It tingles. I can feel our bond." Sniffling, I tap my sternum. "I can feel you here. That is... new." As in, has never happened before. As in, I haven't been bonded until this moment.

Whatever Bogen did to me was pure deceit. A dream.

That deceptive evil toad.

And I fell for it, understood lies to be the truth. I'm still foggy on how to fight it, but I'm going to fight it. What else has he placed in my mind? The old king is dead unless Bogen has a Boggart who can stay shifted when dead. We all saw the body, right?

Donovan's lips catch mine, reigniting the discomfort and need in my core. He moves back enough to whisper, "Your mind is on the loose again, love."

I *love* that he calls me love. "It is. Did you see the king buried?"

"Wow. You are really deep in there, aren't you?" He kisses my forehead. "Talk out loud for me."

Thinking about explaining my situation makes me tongue tied and nervous. He can't be okay with the king's death; he's been Typhon's best friend since birth. What if he's setting me up by getting more information? The tie between us throbs as if angered by my thoughts, but I've been misled before—over and over again.

"Aura..." Donovan singsongs my name.

And I burst. "You can't be okay with this. I helped murder the king—unknowingly, yes—but it's not like I came forward. I was placed in the castle like I'm some kind of royal, when I've only been someone who followed my lust into the worst situation like I was a starving crow begging for a snack. The Unseelie gave me everything I didn't deserve, and you gave me hope that I could keep it, you idiot."

"Aura—"

"I don't know how you're okay with this. You shouldn't have such a foolish mate."

He grips under my knee and pulls my leg up so that I can feel the way I stretch around his cock—his getting-harder-by-the-second cock. "So you admit that you're my mate?"

I gently drag my claws down his back and grip his ass. "As many times as I've been deceived, this tie to you is the only thing that feels truly real."

"Good. Because it is real. Fucking finally." His grin is all charm, but he's not acknowledging very clear Unseelie law, and he doesn't know Bogen.

"It won't last, though."

He gives a slow, deep thrust. "Yes, it will."

He honestly believes that. Always so positive. I push up so I can kiss him, because it may be one of the last times. "I'm going to have to answer for my crimes."

"But…" His brows furrow as he thinks, and his hips still. He shakes his head. "They can't—" then his nose scrunches.

I've had a decade to go through every scenario of taking down Bogen and freeing myself in the process. There's not a one where I come out unscathed. "They can and will. Be my mate for now, Donovan."

His eyes narrow, and he dips to take my lips. "We'll find a way."

He fucks me hard, which both elevates and calms the heat.

My body is satisfied enough, but only for a little while. Then, I ride him, staying as close as possible as he groans and hisses at my teasing ways. The playfulness we sometimes have with each other is far more fun when I know I'm not going to push him away moments later. My legs are shaky and sore after I shatter and he fills me again.

For the first time, we drift off in each other's arms. It may be the first time I've ever felt peace.

A whimper wakes me. Morning light comes from the window, and I strain and swivel to check every inch of the room for Bogen. There's no one else here.

"Donovan?" I push at his chest. "Wake up." But he doesn't.

He whines deep in his throat and he's sweating. I pry open his eyelid and his eye rapidly moves, lost in what I can imagine is a horrid dream. Fury burns bright in my chest.

This is Bogen's doing. But why is he pinpointing Donovan? Why not me? I feel more rested than I ever have.

I sit up, unfolding my wings, then I gasp. They're fully healed. "Stronger together." That will make this easier.

After dressing quickly, I kiss Donovan, press my forehead to his, and sniffle. Leaving him hurts every time. "Hang on, mate."

He's going to be angry when he's free, and we're going to use that because he was right; I can't do this without him and the world can't be rid of this monster without me.

I always knew it would come to this, but it still hurts to know my time here is over. Another few minutes breathing him in would be gracious, but if Bogen can kill someone in their dreams, I will never forgive myself.

I give my wings two test flaps, sending a chair toppling and the curtains fluttering about. One look back at my mate, then, I leap.

There are three guards patrolling in the distance.

I don't want to raise alarm, so I tuck my wings and drop to the second level, landing on the roof at a run. I make my way to the king's chambers, but a muffled scream comes from down the hall as I approach. *He wouldn't.* I run to Typhon and Ember's room, knock, then bolt inside.

Both of them lie on the bed, muscles tense. Typhon grumbles and jerks in his sleep, and Ember clutches at the sheets and squeals in her throat.

Bogen is targeting all of my lovers. How is he doing this?

I retreat, sprint toward my room—or what used to be my room—fling open the first drawer, and breathe a sigh of relief. They didn't take away my things. I pick up my mother's dagger. The blade is still wrapped in wax cloth. I strap it to my hip, then write two words in lip paint on the mirror: Klellic Keep. Rushing at the window, I glide into the morning light.

CHAPTER TWENTY

BACK TO THE TIRED POND SCUM

AURALIA

When the guards fly my way, I point to the castle. "Call the head guardians and set up a full perimeter patrol. Vernon and Crillo need to create a secondary ward for backup. The regent king and queen need guarding. They've been hexed by a Boggart, but not for long. And there may be an attack from the Dark Forest at any moment." Or a spill out when all hell breaks loose. This needs to end. When they look in the direction I'm going to be flying, I clap my hands. "Now."

That sends them darting off.

If my father could only see me now—his unmagical daughter commanding the Crown Unseelie guardians like it's her job. *Ha.* The guardians never listened to him, unless instructed to do so by the gentry.

I make haste toward Klellic Keep, flying as fast as I can, too frazzled to enjoy the warm air, agility, and speed I've missed.

Dropping from the skies a few feet from where the portal should be, I walk into the forest, wings tucked. Bogen doesn't need to know I'm healed. That would set off warning signs for him and if I'm going to present myself as a meal on a silver platter, I need to be how he left me—injured.

There's a huge stranger guarding the tree as I approach. The leshy is old, huge, and moss covered. He looks like a man who was dipped in swamp muck and grew a variety of plants.

His voice is as creaky as the dry branches sticking out of his head. "Who are you?"

"Bogen's wife." I smile up at him because it's not a lie. I am his wife, but—if all goes well—I won't be for much longer. "How can you not know that, leshy?"

He tilts his head, assessing me with intelligent dark green eyes. "You're not a monster."

"Depends on who you ask. Will you move, so that I may pass?"

His snort sends a short plume of white mist into the air. "How do I know you're not lying?" Tension weaves through my chest. This being understands.

"Unlike Bogen, I'm unable to lie. It would send me into convulsions and pain. Now move. I'm in heat, and he's going to want a piece of this." I signal to all of me and step past him when he yields with a bow. Before I step through, I turn back to him. "It would be best to stay away from here."

"I am bound by a favor."

I raise an eyebrow. "You're not the only one. Do you know the Unseelie symbol of surrender?" It's a danger to give this much information, but how many creatures are indebted to Bogen, silently cursing his existence? And if I am betrayed? My sarcasm has helped through the rotations, because if the leshy deceives me and speaks to Bogen, my husband would think I was screwing around to make everyone nervous, never thinking that maybe he should be nervous. I'm a mere pet, after all. *Useless.*

The leshy nods and presses two fingers against his chest.

"Good." I turn to the portal. "Keep that in mind and spread the word to those indebted to the Bogeyman."

Was that too bold? *Yes.* But if I play this right, there won't be enough time to get into trouble.

I dart through the portal and glare at the two huge, wrinkly figures guarding the Keep's doors.

Bogen is nervous if he put the trolls on duty. They don't have the attention span to guard for long, but if there's trouble, they're hard to pass with few weak spots to disarm them.

I keep my wings tight against me as I rush forward. The ward I pass through gives me an alarming tingle. Nothing zaps or sends me into unconsciousness, though, so Donovan's magic inside me must not fully ignite whatever wards Bogen has in place.

"Open the doors," I yell at the two dumbass trolls, who recognize me and shove open the entrance.

A few pebbles clink to the ground, adding to the un-swept gravel. This decrepit place will be in shambles if the Unseelie play this right. I should have drawn maps of the areas I've seen, but it's not like I had time to relay the information while going through my heat. Plus Donovan scouted when he came to find me; he knows what's in store.

I rush the halls, making a quick pause in the kitchen.

Hurna's eyes widen before they run to me and hug my leg. "Why here?"

"I had some unfinished business," I say, pressing a hand to their back. "And if we're very lucky, we may have a battle on our hands soon."

They tilt their head and glance back at the other kitchen staff. "Battle?"

"Wouldn't that be grand? Do you know what this means?" I press my fingers to my sternum.

Hurna's big golden eyes widen further and they nod.

I smile. "Good. Lay low maybe. Do you know where Bogen's room is? He's up to no good right now." I wasn't privy to his whereabouts.

Hurna gives me quick and quiet directions, then runs toward a small door next to shelves lined with mushrooms and roots, and the rest of the kitchen occupiers follow—hopefully to escape. Brownie kin are not fighters.

I grab an abandoned biscuit, because I'm not stupid, and run toward Bogen's room.

A tailed demon guards the hall until it recognizes me and snorts, side-stepping to reveal a door.

I knock, then burst into his room.

"No enter." The rumbly creature that greets me isn't Bogen. It's another Boggart with yellow-tinged skin—the female I thought was his servant. "You!"

I shove the remaining biscuit in my mouth, chewing as I back away. I glance past her to see Bogen in a trance.

The green is gone from his skin, and only a pale gray remains. His breathing comes in short pants, and his head gives shaky jerks. That's going to stop.

I look back at the female blocking my path. "Yep. Me. The wife. And who are you?"

Her grin is malicious. "We don't give secrets to pets."

My fingers slide over the outline of the dagger's hilt under my shirt. I only have one shot though and I'm unlikely to strike the exact place I need to without her being able to take me out too. I hum as if agreeing with her. "Since when do Bogen's servants know secrets?"

The folds on her cheeks darken and puff. "Who told you that?" She's protectively standing in front of Bogen—not like she's been assigned to do so, but as if she wants to be there.

I tilt my head. "Are you his mate?"

Her thin lips tip up like she's been waiting for this moment forever. *I knew it.* "Piteous one of our children will be from such ugly pet. Sit on floor and wait 'til he returns from dreamwalk."

No. I don't know if I can take her—she's even larger than he is, and I'd lose the chance to take him out as well, but this might be the only chance I have.

I grip the hilt when Bogen yells and lists sideways—thank the goddess.

He can't connect with others if he's out of his trance.

I nearly cheer, except she just implied that I'd be producing a child for them and would probably be dead or living in the dungeon until my next heat, while two Boggarts raise my spawn to be the worst fae in the realm. That will not happen if everything goes right today. Which means my dagger will remain sheathed until the exact opportunity.

Hopefully, the nightmares Bogen placed weren't too damaging, and everyone puts the pieces together then checks my room when Donovan tells them I'm missing.

Bogen pushes himself up and speaks in a language I'm not familiar with.

The female responds with something whiny and sharp. After another few words, she shoves past me. The door slams and there's a roar in the hall. Something heavy and metallic clatters against stone.

I furrow my brow and blink several times, attempting to gather some tears. "Are you... cheating on me?" Not laughing is difficult. Donovan's cum is sticky on my thighs.

"Of course not." Has he ever spoken a truth? "Pay no attention to her. She knows nothing." Wheezing his breath, he pushes himself up to his big, flat feet. "You were with one of them, weren't you, Auralia?"

Chapter Twenty-One

ONE NIGHTMARE AFTER ANOTHER

DONOVAN

I jerk from the dream like I'm breaking from an ocean wave. Neither is enjoyable in the least. I fall out of the bed, gasping for air and checking my eyes for damage. With a groan, I cover my face with both hands and try to rub the remnants of raven nightmares off my chilled skin so I can focus. Auralia had been commanding them to attack the castle and everyone in it. So much death.

"Fuck," I grumble and glance around. "Aura?" Why can I never wake up with her? I stagger to the bathroom to see if she's bathing. Empty. There's an itch in my soul—a need to be near my mate and also a dread that something is off beyond a vivid nightmare. I tug on pants and leap from the window, flying down to the second story entry to the royal wing.

There's a lot of patrol out. Maybe Typhon and Ember gave orders because of Auralia's heat.

The halls are bustling with activity, and I halt Gentry Vemmi to ask what's going on.

"We're prepping for war." He grins like this is the most exciting day and flies off before I can ask what the fuck is happening.

My dread skyrockets. I leap to the air, gliding above the busy hallways as I make my way to the royal bedrooms.

Hales and Morti guard Typhon and Ember's chamber.

I land in front of them. "What's going on?"

Hales steps aside. "They wouldn't wake. But now..." He tilts his head toward the carved door. Though it's muffled, Ember gasps and Typhon growls.

With an eye roll, I step in. "You know, I hear there's an incoming war..." I tilt my head, watching Typhon, in full Unseelie rage, rut against Ember like it's his only job in the world. "And I can't find Auralia."

Ember arches her tits upwards, and her head falls farther past the edge of the bed, the tips of her wavy hair brushing the floor. "Typhon needed comforting," she gasps out between thrusts. Her neck has a fresh bite that's weeping crimson.

"Why?" I step closer to take in my friend's bright red eyes and bared fangs. "You're not in heat, are you, Ember?" I take one step back.

"Dreams," he growls. "Raven attack. Everyone. Dead. Ember—" He licks her neck.

Tension rocks through me. "They were pecking everyone apart? Was Auralia there?"

"Stop talking about it." Crying out, Ember digs her nails into Typhon's shoulder.

My dick twitches. I need Auralia now.

Typhon's thrusts go off-rhythm as he comes. He rests his forehead against her neck.

Ember looks upside down at me with bright yellow eyes. "I had the same one, I think. Auralia was a witch, commanding them. Did you say war?"

"So you haven't been briefed?"

They both look at me and ask, "What?"

I give a frustrated growl and turn to the door. "I had the same damn dream. It's Bogen, and I'd wager he has my mate."

"Whoa, whoa, wait, Don—"

I lose the rest of Typhon's words as I step into the hallway and tap Morti's armored chest. "Brief me on everything that has occurred in the last few hours. Keep up." I glide to Auralia's room and halt at the words on the mirror. The invitation when I thought she was abducted only stokes my anger.

She left me... again.

I jerk open the top drawer of her dresser. Her mother's dagger is missing. A lot of emotion boils in my blood—rage, concern, disappointment, and a bunch of plans for punishment when I get my hands back on my mate.

Morti talks to me, pretending I'm not turning into rage incarnate in front of his eyes, and tells me Auralia gave the summons for a defensive double-line war tactic. As soon as I dart back into the hallway, Typhon and Ember sidle up beside me.

"She left?" Typhon asks, then grabs my wrist, dragging me through the narrow passage leading downstairs to the arsenal.

"Yeah. And she's armed. That dagger has a hidden line of iron. I hate that she's even carrying it."

Hales and Morti follow, continuing to give all the information about what everyone is doing in the castle.

Everyone except for Auralia, because she flew off. Did she make the strategy call that would protect us and then run so she wouldn't have to face what she's done? I can't believe she went back to Bogen.

I stop short in the hallway, making Morti bump into my wings. "You said Typhon and Ember couldn't be awoken?"

The rest of the group stops on the stairs.

"Yeah." Morti glances past me to Typhon. "We yelled, slapped you both—apologies—and tried to wake you with crushed corpse lily petals. Nothing."

It all snaps together and my fangs drop. "Bogen targeted Auralia's lovers, not her. She couldn't wake us." I start back down the stairs, pushing us into a run. "That Boggart is done."

"She's with him?" Typhon asks.

I nod. "He knows every trigger she has and is skilled at manipulating her. He'd know that if she was with us, she would go back to him to stop him from hurting us."

We cover ourselves in bark armor and helmets.

Ember, being the smallest and probably most magical of us all, refuses the armor. "I can't move in that, and it will distract me from casting."

Typhon reluctantly agrees and sends Morti and Hales off to alert the guardians to our new plan.

Which leaves two more things to do.

Telling Typhon about what happened to his father will not go well, and the other is probably not the smartest of moves, but setting an assassin loose into a darkling hovel will be entertaining, if not helpful.

I clear my throat. "Auralia told me something—the reason she's indebted to Bogen and here at the castle. It won't be easy to hear."

Typhon shoves a scimitar into his belt sheath. "And we need to know this now?"

"If you don't hear it now, you're going to hear it from Bogen; and I'd rather have your reaction away from Auralia."

Chapter Twenty-Two

EVADE. EFFRONT. EVISCERATE.

AURALIA

Bogen stalks me down the hallway. "I'm losing my patience, pet."

I'd make fun of the threat, but I don't think he's lying for once.

"I just need a biscuit, Bogen. You know how I get when I'm under-fed."

"You haven't told me where they took you."

I dart into the kitchen, which is empty. I'm happy the others are out, and also terrified, because we're alone.

Bogen doesn't seem to want others to see him with me, which is why I hoped taking this party out of the bedroom would help me avoid any kind of mating he's got in mind and give me a chance to stab him in the heart. I'm positive I can do that now that I know he's not my mate. If the right moment happens. I need his eyes off me.

"You don't want to tell me," he grumbles.

Grabbing a biscuit, I put a table between us. "There. This is exactly what I needed."

"Answer, pet. Where did they take you? Who was it? Did they scream?" The monster sounds so amused.

How long will it take Donovan to gain his senses and realize that he needs to get here and go haywire on these monsters with me? His magic tingle in my soul, reassuring me that even if Bogen wore a Donovan glamour, I'd know he was false the moment I looked in his eyes. I wish I was looking at my mate right now. I've been stalling forever and the ache to be near him is getting to me.

I take a bite and slowly chew, holding my finger up to tell him to wait while I swallow, though the delicious food feels like a rock in my stomach. "They took me to the Unseelie Court, Bogen. I thought you'd have known and come after me."

"Why go after you when I knew you'd come back?" His bulging eyes narrow, and he looks at my tucked wings.

I need a diversion before he questions how I got here so quickly. Shrugging, I finish the biscuit. "I mean, it was up in the air there for a bit. My bed there is very comfortable, and you're not exactly known for being a hospitable host. Besides these, of course." When I reach for another biscuit, he swipes his hand, sending the tray flying across the kitchen.

I raise an eyebrow. "Quite the waste."

"Yes, *you* are. Tell me what they're planning. Have they spoken of a heat wave?"

"A heat wave? What's that?" It has to be of interest, because he's acting completely off. Though, maybe that was from inhabiting at least three Unseelie's dreams.

He bares his teeth. "So they haven't. Interesting. I would think they'd have caught wind of more, but it appears they're just as useless as you."

"Well, you handpicked me, so what does that say about you?"

There's a tug in my chest; like a warning, but with flutters replacing the dread.

Bogen takes that moment to leap on the kitchen table and crouch, making me scurry backwards. "Are you in heat yet, pet? If we're lucky, we'll get two chances. An Nasc Iontach is rare."

I know that phrase from somewhere. An old account from an early-century scroll, I think. "The great bonding," I whisper.

"How have you heard of it?"

I shrug, not about to tell him I've read as many fae history books as I could get my hands on.

He squints his bulgy eyes. "Surprising. Are you in heat, Auralia? Answer."

Now is my last trick. I only hope Donovan is close, or I'm royally fucked in multiple ways.

I put my palms on the table. "You can't tell?"

His flappy cheeks puff. Maybe I went too far there.

I roll my eyes. "Yes, Bogen. It started before I was taken from this keep. I'm achy." Slightly. It's mainly passed, but whether it be from the tail end of the heat or all the sex Donovan and I had, I do ache. I lean in, though it disgusts me, and inhale against the folds of Bogen's neck. He doesn't smell bad exactly. But he certainly doesn't smell like mine. I feel nothing between us but repulsion. "Being near you should strengthen it, right?"

"Yes." He raises an eyebrow in an expression that may be sexy for a Boggart. "Get up here, on the table, and lie down. On your stomach."

And here is where things are going to get tricky. *Do not piss off the Boggart; he will realize what you're doing and find a punishment you haven't considered yet.*

I crinkle my nose. "In the kitchen? Why?"

"So we can mate."

It turns out I can smile, even when completely repulsed. "But I want to face you." *So I can stab you in your withered, cold heart.*

"I don't want to look at you." He reaches for me, and I take one step back.

"That could be very hurtful, Bogen." I take a quick step sideways and set off to explore the expansive room. I need to stall. "Not very mately of you."

"Take your trousers off."

Picking up a knife from one of the counters, I glare at him over my shoulder. "So you can make fun of my curves again? I'd rather not." I clean my nails with the blade while he watches every move I make from his table perch. "You know, I'm not really feeling in heat right now. Maybe it will kick in later." When my mate shows up.

"Now."

I pout my lip. "What if I have a headache?"

"You won't have your head if you don't obey."

I slam the knife down and throw my hands in the air. "Fine, Bogen. But can you..." I swish my hand at him. "Change into something more decent?" I point at him. "Not the duke. Maybe... hm." I tap my chin. "The king?" My heart hurts too much for him to toy with Donovan's image, and he will expect me to choose a lover.

Bogen glares. "You are the most fortunate being in the realm, pet. I wouldn't do this for any other." What a joke. The only moments of fortune I've had were when I got my hands on that heat suppressor, when the Unseelie Crown Court accepted me into their ranks, and then when I bonded with Donovan.

Bogen begins his shift, and I nearly cheer as the image of Kage stands on the table, panting.

It's impressive and makes me miss my friend—the way I'd make fun of his beloved glossy hair until he'd pout at me. He taught me the slyest sarcasm, and how to hold a straight face when diplomarians demanded the most ridiculous things, like moving a lake closer to their keep. With those thoughts, a wave of sadness rolls through me. I'm not sure I'll ever see the real him again. If I do, it will be at my sentencing and execution.

"This does not make you ready?" Bogen asks.

I shake my head. "The other king, *husband*. Oh, well, I suppose he's still the prince, but the interim king. Try him."

Bogen stills and tilts his head at me, assessing me with Kage's green eyes. "Are you attempting to play me for a fool, pet?"

It's possible I carried a tone.

With the best timing ever, there's a yell and a scuffle down the hall.

Bogen turns away from me.

I grab the knife from the counter and surge forward with my wings. Baskets and utensils hit the ground from the wind thrust. I jam the blade into the Kage mimic's back all the way to the hilt, stomach churning at the pop through muscle. That will weaken him.

A screech comes from Bogen, but another comes from my right. I turn, pulling my mother's dagger and unwrapping the wax cloth to reveal the deadly-to-fae blade.

The female—Bogen's real mate—comes from the now-empty corner where there had been a large, woven basket, ruining my opportunity for another stab. I really dislike Boggarts and their sneaky ways. The female snarls, and I hold my knife out, gliding backward toward the open kitchen door. It's hard to navigate with wings. They tap against the ceiling and narrow doorway, veering me off course.

Bogen sneers and makes those odd chirps of communication with his mate. It helps break the feeling that Kage is here. Bogen is not him. He's just a powerful Boggart.

And his damned mate is in my way.

I focus on Bogen's version of Kage that just isn't quite right as I hold off the female with my extended blade. "Interesting that I can stab you, isn't it, *husband*? Looks like we don't have as strong of a bond as I thought."

Bogen shrugs and the kitchen knife falls from his back. He doesn't seem any worse for wear as he moves forward, arms in front, blocking his chest. "We'll amplify your heat. You will give me what I want."

"Or not." I leap to the air, but after one flap, he surges forward, grabbing my ankle. I crash into the ground, kick him and scramble backward.

He lurks forward. "How did your wings heal?"

More yells sound in the distance.

The Unseelie are coming. I have backup for the first time, and it makes me too bold.

I smile. "Because I'm mated and much stronger."

Bogen narrows his eyes at me. "You've been a terrible pet, Aura. You'll pay for that heavily." He drops his arms to his side as if I'm not a threat at all.

I focus on the point of his chest and hope there's a heart in there. "Another day maybe, you foul wretch of a fae."

The female screeches as I throw my dagger and, so unfortunately, it strikes perfectly into her chest as she throws herself in front of her mate. That was not meant for her. Her scream is long and bubbly as she crashes to the ground. Bogen squeals and drops down beside her.

Leaping, I glide to the kitchen doors as he howls in rage and loss. I should feel guilt or pity, but all I feel is stark terror as he bellows, "Auralia," because I just used my only weapon to kill his mate, and I know what I'd do if I were in his place...

I'd make it hurt.

CHAPTER TWENTY-THREE

DEATH TO ALL WHO HARBOR HERE

DONOVAN

A quarter of the beings we encounter give us the hand signs of surrender, making things confusing, yet clear. Auralia had to have alerted them at some point.

A spray of blood streaks my face as Jinora slashes a path through a line of armed kobold guards with a set of finger daggers she had stashed under the floorboards in her room. And I thought Auralia could be vicious.

The Grimm Brothers hold back, watching over the fight, measuring us up. It may have been too much to call in the most dangerous of the Enforcers, but we couldn't take a chance with, not only Auralia on the line, but our entire court.

We've been infiltrated, and they've been building an empire in this old keep.

Jinora stabs a thin female pixie in both shoulders and holds her in place as she screams. "Where are prisoners kept?"

"I like her," Ash, the more jovial of the brothers, says before moving beside Jinora and gripping the pixie by her hair. "Yes, fiend. Where are the prisoners kept? Are there any dangerous ones?"

I don't have time to listen, because a group of what could be guardians enters the main hall. The creatures we're fighting are a mix of small dark fae—seemingly the angriest of pixies, kobolds, leprechauns, and even a few nymphs that look as though they're wasting away. They probably lost their trees.

I cut down an incoming pixie and a crackling ball of lightning flies by my left ear, crashing into the three that were behind him, sending them screeching off in all directions.

"Good shot, Ember," I yell and fly forward, pushing our group into the narrow, crumbling passageway the enemy has been arriving from.

The state of this place is sad. I'd been inside the Sidhe's underground lair twice when I was a youngling while my father presented them with territory warnings. The keep didn't look like this. It had been clean before and had smelled of bark and bergamot incense. The scent now is acrid.

I believe now more than ever that Bogen forced Auralia into this place and she felt she had no choice but to return. We should have paused and looked into things further before annihilating the Sidhe, even if they'd always been a threat. Our retribution helped a bigger threat, and I'd wager Bogen set it all up.

But I bet he didn't expect this.

"You look ready to tear down the building," Typhon says beside me, but maintains his distance as we go deeper into the keep. It's too quiet for my liking.

I nod. "We didn't even question the Sidhe before we took them out. We assumed the worst and acted on it." I glance his way, and the red in his eyes settles my anger. He's as riled up as I am. "If we would have called for a meeting instead of a slaughter, we could have saved Aura far earlier than now." I rub at the ever-present ache in my chest. *Mine.*

"There's no revoking the past. Should we not invade now?"

"He has my mate, and even if he didn't, he's too dangerous to the fae realm. But the others—the ones surrendering or those caught up like Aura—they stay safe. Who knows how many innocent fae we took that day out of fury."

"I wish Kage were here." Typhon looks forward, at the dark entrance to the main hall. "He'd know what to do. How to…" Typhon scrunches his nose.

"There's no fixing any of this. Just halting a serious problem."

"The Bogeyman ends today." Ember flies in behind us, her iridescent wings buzzing in the small space. She lifts her hands and light pours from her palms. She closes her eyes, inhales, then throws the ball into the next room.

Shrieks pierce the air.

I nod. "So that was supposed to be an ambush."

"And now, it isn't. Shall we?"

Claws replace my nails, and I settle deeper into the monstrous Unseelie nature. "We shall."

We fly in a stacked position into the room—Jinora and the Grimm Brothers leading on the ground; the rest of us hovering above. As the group clashes with the army below, we pause over the armed crowd.

Typhon pulls his scimitar. "You were holding out on us, dark ones. You may leave if you disagree with Bogen's ways."

There's a shout of, "King Bogen," on the ground to my right.

I dive, gripping the creature's throat and lifting him, dodging two blades. "Where is he and his—" It feels so wrong to even consider my words. "Wife."

The kobold is gray and round and attempts to stab me with a dagger that I smack out of its hand. "Magic," it squeals, and the world spins, revealing the night sky and empty fields.

I'm holding a thick branch in my hand, which I glare at and squeeze harder. "I'm not a youngling. Tell me where she is, little tree."

Glamours are amazing and annoying. I've never come close to mastering anything that looks remotely realistic. Ember, however, is a glamour powerhouse and is hopefully fixing this mess as our mages are back at the castle, casting a full web of wards against both darklings and other Unseelie courts as we're here and not there. There's protocol and rules, but the ones we called to help us are the most dangerous and, one day, they may decide not to play by those rules.

The limb whimpers.

"Say it," I whisper. "Don't die for him."

"Long. Live. The. Ki—"

I squeeze harder and a chilling crack interrupts the silence of the false night. I chuck the limp tree branch into the fields. Then I inhale deep, and roar.

The world wavers, then falls away, and as my vision clears, a fist approaches and connects, sending a shot of pain through the side of my head.

So they have a troll, I consider as I fly through the air and into the crowd below.

Someone stabs me in the shoulder, and that is enough. If they're on our side, they're no longer here.

I let loose, lashing out with claws and fangs. Sour blood spills over my tongue, enraging me further. I elbow, slash, and kick. I even forget I have a dagger because my body is enough. My Unseelie nature gets lost in the blood, and I allow it to ride over me to release some of this tension of being separated from my mate. I work my way to another door, all while yelling for Auralia, when a strangely familiar face arrives in the doorway.

Typhon yells first. "Kage!"

I notice several things at once. No one is attacking him. And the king is bloodied. His green eyes are odd—vacant maybe, or just...not right. Auralia's dagger is in his hand.

"Ty!" I yell. "Wait."

But he doesn't.

CHAPTER TWENTY-FOUR

THIS IS REALLY GOING TO HURT

AURALIA

From behind Bogen, I take in the room, lit by two of Ember's light balls, to see what my next play will be.

The guardian's fight the kobolds with little fuss, except for the few Unseelie clearly lost in a glamour as they stab the Keep's walls or stay still in the air, waiting for an out of whatever the few magical beings have created to distract them. Screams come from the back corner, and my blood runs cold.

There are two massive Unseelie—The Grimm Brothers. The darkest of Unseelie don't come out for just any battle. They're the annihilators—the ones nicknamed after the darkest of legends because they are the terrors in the night. Did Donovan, Typhon, and Ember call them for me? That was too dangerous. They will want something in return.

Bogen jerks at the shackles again, sending another sharp stab of pain into my wrists. He's still disguised as Kage. He's kept the image on purpose, because he does everything on purpose, and I'm sad to say one of my theories was correct. As soon as Bogen steps into the light, Typhon appears rocked—his red eyes fading to gray, face so hopeful as he spots what he thinks is his brother.

Bogen chuckles, but it sounds more like himself, because I don't believe he's ever been close enough to Kage to hear his laugh and copy it. "We were going to leave, pet—escape out the back. But then you had to…" His whispered voice turns into a whimper. "But don't worry. I'm going to pay you back, then we'll go. I will torture you for decades for what you've done."

I cringe. "You've already tortured me for a decade. Just stab me and get it over with."

"No. You have a long, painful life ahead of you, starting now. I'll make sure of it."

Fortunately, Bogen thinks Kage is the most powerful of the Crown Unseelie, but Kage is powerful with words. Typhon and Donovan are warriors, and with Ember and the Grimm Brothers in the mix? Even if Bogen somehow survives this, his followers won't.

I grip the chain Bogen's holding and jerk, hoping Typhon sees it, because Kage would never shackle me. Not even in a fun way, because he doesn't mix pleasure and court business, which could be why he has stayed with the nymphs. The Unseelie king needed to get fucked.

"Ty! Wait!" Donovan darts from the ground, distracting him from Bogen.

Seeing my mate makes my heart skip a beat. He's coated in blood, making my fangs drop farther.

Bogen glares over his shoulder at me. Typhon is bound to realize this isn't his brother, because Kage could never look this vicious. "I doubt they can hear you over the noise, but if you scream, I'll take your wings entirely off instead of opening them."

That would be cruel, but taking Donovan, Typhon, and Ember out of the world would be the worst he could do to me.

A squad of pixies rain down on my friends and my mate.

I pull at the chains again, hoping to distract Bogen, so he doesn't see how well they fight.

He spins, drops the chain, and nails me with a backhand that throws me against the wall.

I gasp and rub what feels like fire across my cheek.

He turns back to the room of war and yells, "There are so many of these kobolds to crush, am I right? I'm holding them off through this passage. Come help me."

I can only gain a glance around Bogen in the narrow space, but I can see Typhon approaching with his weapon lowered. He won't realize the danger until it's too late. It will only take one well-placed stab from my mother's blade to make us a kingless court. I have to do something drastic, chip away at Bogen, because he won't expect it.

Then I remember the old wartime scrolls.

This will not end well for me, but I knew that long ago. I have one shot—a warrior's ending play.

My mate will finish what I start.

This is really going to hurt, but if Bogen decides to follow through on his threats, I won't have this chance again.

Ignoring the throb in my face and shoulder, I let the darkness of my nature settle over me, lean back against the wall, wrap my left wing around me, then bite. The pain is sharp. Before I can think about how much worse it's going to be, I lock down my jaw and jerk, breaking my wing tips open to reveal the razor-sharp blade of bone underneath soft leathery skin.

The pain is dazzling and I lean, breathing hard, and fighting to focus without making too much sound.

My other wing is harder to maim, because I know how the first feels. But I do it because war is upon us, and if I've learned anything in my decade of shame and fear, it's that the worst thing to do is nothing. I won't be useless. The taste of my blood brings bile up my throat, or maybe it's the pain, but I swallow it down and prepare.

"That might not be Kage, Ty," Donovan yells as he flies forward, wrapping an arm around Ty and dragging him backward. "Could be Bogen."

Bogen tenses, and I take the chance to jab my right wing bone into his lower back. As he screams, so do I, because the heat of his body feels like lava against my open flesh.

I shove my other wing through the Kage mimic's side, but run into a hard wall—probably a rib. It's impossible to figure out a shifted Boggart's anatomy. The pain that shocks up my wings and neck makes stars blink as Bogen gives a raspy cry. Hopefully that's enough to show Typhon that this is not his brother.

"No!" Typhon yells, surging forward.

Donovan tackles Typhon, holding him back, though my mate looks likely to throw his king as his eyes flit between the dagger in Bogen's hand and me, now that I'm in the dim light.

I lift my bound hands. "It's Bog—"

Bogen elbows my left wing hard. The crack radiates a deeper pain through my entire body.

I scream as he grips my neck and squeezes, dragging me off him.

He leans close to whisper, "You just wait." He turns back to Typhon, still holding me by the neck. "She attacked me, just like she murdered our father. She's a spy and a traitor."

Gritting my teeth, I jam the wing he didn't break back in a little higher. Tears make my vision wavy until they spill over.

Ember approaches, holding a ball of lightning in both palms.

Bogen buckles forward, baring his teeth as a quiet squeal sounds in his throat. Then he raises the dagger toward me, but I know he won't do it. He needs me for his plan. It's the others he wants to lure closer.

"Stay back," I rasp. There's so little air in my lungs. "Dagger. Iron."

"Let her go." Donovan hovers beside Typhon, no longer needing to hold him back. My mate's eyes stay on me, flitting as he takes in my face, Bogen's—or Kage's—hand around my throat and my mangled wings.

"How did she kill him?" Typhon asks.

The shame of the past hits me hard. I struggle for breath so I can explain, but it's no use, so I shove my wing in deeper, only making Bogen appear more annoyed, even if the Kage glamour is turning a pale green.

Bogen squeezes harder. "She led him to the Sidhe. There are more down that hall lying in wait. They will take us all out, brother, unless we attack first. Go. I will handle this traitor."

"Is that enough, *brother?*" Donovan growls, inching forward.

Oh. Kage calls Typhon "Tuber" because he told him he was born from the ground like a root vegetable and that's why Typhon's magic is what it is. I've never heard Kage call him "brother" in all the years I've been at the castle.

"I'm ready," Donovan says. The dagger Bogen holds too close to my face begins to bend toward Bogen, until it's sharply curved.

"Hurry, brother." Fortunately, Bogen has his eyes on Typhon. "Or help me finish Auralia if that's what you want. Hurry. She's dangerous."

"Ember," Typhon whispers.

There's an explosion of light and a screech. I scream too because Bogen is dragged off my wing, leaving it searing in the chilly air.

Darkness invades my vision in pulses, but I'm able to catch a glimpse of Donovan, Ty, and the Grimm Brothers ripping apart Bogen in a way that would fill our most vicious Unseelie ancestors with gruesome admiration.

Guardians surround the carnage, ready to block any escape.

"Your wings," Ember says, dropping in next to me.

I give her a weak smile. "Are not my biggest concern. You know about the previous king's death?"

She nods. "Donovan explained."

"Then that's that." I curl into the pain, keeping my mangled wings as extended as possible as I rest my head on Ember's thigh. "There are protocols."

"I know. They would be different if you were Seelie."

I nod. "Banishment?"

"Yes." She runs her fingers through my tangled hair. "We don't do well alone."

"Donovan won't do well when I'm gone."

"Don't go that far yet, Aura. You've done a lot for this kingdom. That counts. I can't believe you kept all this to yourself. You must have felt alone for a very long time."

"Since I met the Bogeyman." I close my eyes, unseating a stream of tears. "And even before that. I thought he was a dream come true, not my worst nightmare."

"You're not alone anymore." She shifts from under me, propping my shoulder against the stone wall. "And your mate is coming, so I'm going to back away because he's looking rather lethal." She flutters backwards just as Donovan's blood splattered face appears in front of me.

He clenches his jaw tight as he looks over me, then reaches out to lift my chin. "Never again, mate."

CHAPTER TWENTY-FIVE

A NEW SCHEME

DONOVAN

I would do irrational things to heal my mate—call upon the gods, or take her to the Lady of the Lake and beg. I'd cut off my own wings and fuse them to hers if that were a thing. It's not.

"I can't believe you did that," I whisper, looking over Auralia's ripped open, broken wings. "That was an ending blow strategy." One only used when there were no other options to stay alive, except to take an enemy along with you through the veil.

Her breaths come in a quick cadence, but she grins. "Look at you, studying your Unseelie ancient history."

"I had to keep up with you. There were only so many times I would allow myself to look foolish in front of you because I didn't know something that easily fell from your beautiful lips." I'm not sure how to touch her without causing her more pain.

"I had to have something, if not magic. Knowledge it was." Eyes fluttering closed, she rests back against the cave wall as the screams and sounds of death grow less frequent. "He's dead, right?"

"As long as he can't be alive while in pieces, the hauntings of the Bogeyman are through."

Her eyebrows furrow, and she swallows. Tears are imminent and I can't not touch her.

I pull her into me and stand as carefully as I can. "Relax your wings. I'm going to hold them up." I use my magic to bend them so they won't drag and be harmed further as she hisses and presses her bared fangs against my neck. I lift my chin. "You can bite, my love. Anything you want is yours."

She loops her bound wrists over my head. "I want more time with you."

I want that too. I carry Auralia through the main hall, dodging bodies, and catch Typhon's eye.

He sighs, takes Ember's hand and follows us. My best friend doesn't like this situation one bit and I don't envy him; because he's stuck between loyalty to court protocols and loyalty to Auralia and me.

The Grimm Brothers lean against the wall, chatting with each other. Ash's blond waves look closer in color to Corbin's with the blood tinting them.

Pausing in front of them, I tip my head toward the doorway. "Find Jiminadora and her family if they're here, and bring them back to the castle. She needs to go back into her cell in the barracks until..." Kage returns? Typhon sentences her and Auralia? I don't know what's going to happen. "Just find her. We're torching this keep as soon as you're out."

They both nod and leap into flight.

"What do we owe them?" Auralia whispers.

"Not sure yet, but they're acting like they have something in mind, otherwise Corbin would have told me to clean up my own mess."

"My mess."

"Our mess," I correct and walk down the corridor that will get us out of this bad memory.

Typhon sighs at the ceiling as he leans further back in the king's office chair. "You know I can't do that, Donovan. If I let Aura go, then the other four courts will riot and choose another king or queen interim. Do you want Bianca on our throne?"

"Fuck no." I tug at my curls. "And she's due for her annual attempt to snag the crown."

"She is. And Kage isn't even here to reject her attempts."

There's a knock on the door and I stride across the room to open it, thinking it's Ember coming back from talking to Auralia. Our Seelie princess is having a rough time accepting our Unseelie ways, as am I.

But, it's the Grimm Brothers, still bloodied, who slide past me into the office without an invitation.

Corbin veers off and settles against a bookcase in the most dim corner of the room, but Ash throws himself into one of the two cushy chairs, one leg flopped over the arm. "I know something fascinating." He bites his smiling lip. Sometimes I think Corbin, who is the gentry of the Enforcer Court but won't admit it, keeps Ash around to both speak for him and push the buttons of stressed out Unseelie.

Ember steps into the office and crosses her arms. "We have to get your brother back."

"I'm aware," Typhon monotones.

She shakes her head. "Not of this."

"Aw, let me tell them," Ash whines.

Ember taps her sternum. "But Aura told me."

"And Jin filled in the rest," Ash says. "It was a team effort."

Corbin snorts and runs his knuckles across his blood-stained beard.

The rest of us cleaned up, but they were out hunting Jinora.

I shut the door and step next to Ember. "Does this have to do with Auralia?" I'm more than ready to fly down to the dungeon to check on her.

"No." Ash pulls out a weed stick and a flint lighter.

Ember nods. "Yes. It does."

I stare at the stick he places between his lips and use my magic to bend it into a broken twist.

He huffs and glares at me. "You were far more fun when you didn't have a mate."

"Time and place." I snap my fingers three times. "Someone tell us what's going on."

Ash leaps into a sitting position and holds up his finger as Ember opens her mouth. "The nymphs," he says pointedly, before leaning back. "Have a secret—well, not a secret anymore—but few know it. Bogen obviously understood the lore well."

"Jinora knew," Ember says. "And a few of the Brownie kin that followed us here to check on Auralia."

"She's a sweet little thing, isn't she?" Ash sighs. "Jinimadora."

Ember tilts her head and glances over to Corbin. "Didn't she stab you?"

He unsnaps his armor and lifts the tunic underneath to show a slice on his lean side, perfectly placed between leather plates. "Apparently." He shrugs his clothing back into place.

"But who hasn't?" Ash grins.

I ready myself to impatiently explode.

He stands and walks to the window, pushing the curtain aside to take in the morning light. "There are so many fae legends that it's difficult to decipher truth from hope. But when the Bogeyman believes something to be true, we should listen." He tugs the curtain closed and faces us. "It's too early to tell exactly why he made every move he did, but he was working toward a goal—gaining an offspring from Donovan's mate..." He bows his head in respect to my anger. "And to gain another offspring from his true mate, whose parts are also currently burning in the fires of Klellic Keep, courtesy of Auralia. Wicked dagger, by the way. Where did it wander off to?"

I stare blankly at him. "Aura was never mated to him, was she?" I ask.

"No," Ember says. "But he jumped into her dreams for decades to make her believe that was true. Same with Jinora—"

"Jinimadora," Ash corrects.

Ember has an impressive glare for a Seelie, and he pinches his lips.

She touches my arm. "He placed dreams in everyone around her to solidify his plans. And he did the same with many of the fae he forced to be indebted to him."

"He was brilliant." Ash clears his throat when we all glare at him. "A monster, but brilliant. Alright; my turn again. He did all this preparation because an An Nasc Iontach is upon us."

Typhon snorts. "The mystical blessing of the fae gods that happens—what? Every five thousand rotations?"

Ash claps. "That's the one. Though it's something more like the power of threes and alignment of the double blue moon to the North Star—" He swishes his bloodied fingers through the air. "You know how the gods are. So yes, that's upon us."

"And this has to do with Kage because..." Typhon raises his eyebrows.

"Why do you think the nymphs have him?" Corbin murmurs.

My blood chills in my veins.

Typhon's face also goes pale in realization. "Unusual pairings are more likely. They want to gain as many offspring of the Royal Unseelie Court as possible, so they can claim the throne."

"Surprise." Ash wiggles his fingers. "And they have allies, which is why you haven't been able to break the wards. And if you do, any Unseelie that crosses into the territory will be annihilated. Are you ready for this little tidbit?"

"No," I groan. We were hoping for Kage's return any day, but after a full rotation, we'd be able to call for an invasion if there had been no progress. We don't need *tidbits* holding that up.

"Good." He nods. "They have hellhounds on guard. We love those, don't we?"

There are few things that can destroy Unseelie without a fuss. It was said the hellhounds were spawned to guard the dark gods from their own perfect creation, but that could be our vanity getting entwined with lore.

Typhon runs a hand down his face. "Why haven't they destroyed Kage as he's trapped in their territory?"

"Probably an enchanted relic." Corbin tugs a book from the shelf with one finger hooked on the edge of its spine. He tilts his head as he looks at the exposed cover. "Like the alert pendants the Seelie created. He wears it, and they won't eat him." His nose scrunches before he pushes the book back in place, and returns to scowling.

"And let me guess…" I take a step toward the door. "You want the pendant?"

"Yeah," Corbin and Ash say together.

Ash tries to straighten out his weed stick. "For our payment when we assist with taking down the nymph wards. As for the Bogeyman's wards and bloodshed… we have ideas."

"*You* have an idea," Corbin says.

So the brothers aren't entirely united on one payment. That could be an advantage.

Ember walks around the desk and cups Typhon's cheek. "Can we now talk about my plan to get Kage out? We need him for Auralia's trial, and he can't be with a coven of nymphs if the heat wave is real."

He takes her hand and drags her into his lap. "It can't be you. They will kill you if they find out who you are, and I will run through the territory line and get eaten by a hellhound if I'm away from you."

I understand that and take another step to the door.

Ember rests her forehead against his. "Fine. But I have someone who would be perfect. She doesn't have the attachment of a mate—she lost him years ago—but has impressive magic and the strength from that bond is still intact."

CHAPTER TWENTY-SIX

OUR FIRST HOME

AURALIA

Every bit of me hurts. Every. Bit.

I lie on the torture table—also the healing table—and take a deep breath, though my lungs hurt from the panting.

Donovan's footsteps approach from the hall, and I sit up.

"Stop that," the healer says, pushing my shoulder. It takes no effort to get me back in my place. "Do it again and I'm going to make you lie on your stomach."

I flinch from the memory of the painful angle that had put on my wings. At least if I'm on my back, they can relax flat against the table. He returns to putting me back together.

How is she?" Donovan asks, appearing at my side to take my hand.

The healer's black brows furrow so much, there's barely a hair's width between them. "She's obstinate."

"Rude," I whisper.

He presses more plant glue into my frayed wing skin and pinches. "And strong. She's only passed out twice so far."

I bare my fangs. "It turns out, cleaning guts off bone shards is more painful than breaking them open. Now I know."

Donovan kisses my forehead and then my lips. "Always seeking knowledge."

That makes me laugh, then whimper as the movement reignites the pain coursing through my entire body.

"Hold still," the healer grumbles. "I'm almost done."

The pain is easier with Donovan near. He leans on the table and talks to me like we're at dinner or how I'd like to think we'd be in bed, if I hadn't run out the door once our baser needs were met every time we've been together. We won't have that opportunity, which is unfortunate.

"How long do I have?" I whisper to Donovan.

His eyebrows furrow. "How long for what?"

"Execution day."

The healer wraps my wing without a pause, and Donovan puts his attention on the wall. Both of them know the rules. We all do.

Donovan threads his fingers through my hair. "That was an archaic law."

"One that hasn't changed."

After a tuck of gauze that makes me jerk, the healer stands. "I'm done for now. Do you need an escort to return Auralia to her cell?"

Donovan slides his arms under my back and knees and lifts me. "No, I think we can manage." He carefully navigates through the doorway and into the hall toward the prisoner holding area. "There's nothing we can do without Kage here, so for now..." He trails off and smiles, looking forward.

I follow his line of sight and gasp. The cell I've been kept in now has a curtain that's pulled back with a golden tassel, revealing my bed from upstairs, my dresser, a small table with two full plates of food and what looks to be a bottle of wine. Someone has squeezed a small tub into the corner of the room. "What is that?"

"Our first home—or room. It's where we're staying until we can get Kage back, and he can hear your entire story and then petition to change the laws. Until then, there's a stay of execution and if anyone disagrees, I'll rip their head off." He kisses my slack, parted lips. "Since I already did that to Bogen, I think my reputation will keep the pro-testors at bay."

"But... it was Kage's father." I swallow hard. "Ty won't even look at me, which is understandable. I can't expect Kage to do anything different. Why would he pardon me for what happened?"

He steps into the cell that now smells of fruit and flowers and sets me on my feet, turning me to face him. "Because you were forced into the situation just like twenty-nine others. They will speak for you."

"What?"

His eyes are warm and mischievous. "Silly Unseelie, thinking you didn't make allies along the way." He wraps me up in his arms and I need a million touches like this. "You are so loved."

A hot tear spills from my eye. I have to bite my tongue to keep more at bay.

Donovan kisses my neck. "Let's eat and settle in."

Sure enough, a couple of Hurna's legume cakes spotlight on the plate. "Hurna's here?"

"Of course they are. Them and an unsettling amount of kitchen staff. There were a lot of favors and secrets in play that you freed everyone from." Before I can protest, or deny what he's trying—overtly—to say, his hand wanders over my hip. "Are you through your heat?"

With a grin, I turn in his arms. "If I say 'no,' will you fuck me hard while I eat this amazing food?"

He scoffs, face twisting up in insult. "What kind of mate would deny you that?" He tugs at the wrap I'm wearing. "Actually, I would because you're healing. I'll fuck you slowly and carefully."

EPILOGUE

AURALIA

"Did you sleep well?" Donovan asks, just like he does each morning.

It's been a moon since Klellic Keep burned to the ground. I don't dream anymore, and I'm unsure if my mind is just taking a needed rest or if Bogen stole that part of me for good when he died. But each day I've unwound a little more, even with the concern of what will happen when Kage returns.

Reaching back, I ruffle Donovan's curls. "No dreams."

"Are your wings better today?" My mate's voice is raspy and a little growly.

I wiggle my bare ass against his hard erection. "You want to touch them, don't you?"

"So bad, love." He runs his fangs over my neck. So it's going to be that kind of morning. "It's been too long since I've held you down using them." Oh, havoc's elixir... My mistake—it's going to be *that* kind of morning. "Say it," he whisper-growls, claws scoring the tender flesh of my hip. "If you're carrying my child, we may not be able to play like this for much longer."

"You're going to treat me like glass, aren't you?" Pinching his ear, I move his head back and forth.

He nips at my wrist. "No, love. You've proved you're made of diamond. Play with me."

I will deny him nothing for the rest of my days. "Only if you can catch me." I elbow him and leap from the bed as he curses. It's a tiny room that we're locked in, so it's not like he won't capture me, but that doesn't make this game any less tantalizing. I slide behind the curtains, wrapping myself in them in case Jinora can see us from her cell. It doesn't take but a moment for Donovan to tug them from my grasp.

I duck and slip out the other side, gliding across the room. I hope I get the chance to fly again because my wings ache to stretch out fully and grasp the air. As soon as I land, Donovan grips my hair, making a tightness tingle along my scalp.

He pulls me against him, skin hot against mine. "Is that all you've got, mate?"

I spin, crawling up his hard body and planting a rough kiss to his lips.

"Aura." He groans and grips my ass, then shoves me against the wall. "You never play fair."

"Where's the fun in that?" I twist and shove, twirling from his grip and racing the few steps to the other side of the room. With a leap, I roll over the bed, putting it between us, but Donovan is close and makes a grab for me. I take a step back and hiss, though I smile as I look over his body and impressive erection. My heart races at the feral look in his red eyes. "I've always loved being chased by you."

He hums. "And I've always loved catching you." He comes around the side, leaving me with one path—the bed.

I wait until he jumps, then I scramble over the tousled sheets, but he snags my foot and jerks, sending me crashing face down on the mattress. He smacks my ass hard before gripping each of my wings right where they meet my back. The rough squeeze he gives them makes tension hit my clit.

"Hurt?" he whispers.

"No." My entire body tingles, starting from where he's holding me.

He growls, telling me to prepare for the best time. "Spread wide for me."

My breaths come in short gasps as I let my knees slide over the mattress.

He tugs me into position, making me arch, then he gathers both wing bases in one hand and grips my breast in a punishing hold. "So my good mate does know how to behave." The way he licks my neck is both sweet and possessive, and I grow wet between my legs.

"Stop teasing me, Donovan."

With the pad of his thumb, he toys with my nipple. "But we love that, don't we?"

He's not wrong. I whimper at the spike of pleasure he stirs in me. "Just get on with it, lover."

The chuckle against my neck is dark and mischievous. His grip tightens on my wings, but he lets go of my breast to line the head of his cock against my entrance. Planting his palm on the mattress, he sinks his fangs into the spot where my neck meets my shoulder as he thrusts in. I cry out at the unexpected surge of pleasure and pain. I'm held fast as he rails against me. When an Unseelie's wings are held like this, it's difficult to do much else except take it.

And take it I do. I tilt my hips to get him deeper.

The slide of his cock's piercings builds that pleasured-ache into a tight coil of need.

As if he knows exactly what I need, he retracks his fangs, licks my neck, then lets go of my wings to cup my face, turning my head to make me look at his intense gaze.

"Tell me you're mine, Auralia. No matter what, who, or where..." He stares at my lips, moving so close, his heat soaks into me. His eyes meet mine again. "You. Are. Mine."

I'm breaking inside in the most delicious way. "I'm yours, Donovan. And you're mine."

"Damn right I am." He sits up to flip me over, and slides back between my legs, which I wrap around his hips, tugging him to put his weight on me.

We fall into our rhythm—our new rhythm—one that is both hard and sweet, and passionately violent. I rip the sheets above my head with my claws when I come, and Donovan curses so loud, I'm sure anyone in the three floors above us heard him. He tucks his face against my neck as we catch our breath.

"Do you think Jinora heard us?" he whispers.

I grin so wide. "I think the guardians at the Enforcer Court heard us."

He nuzzles his nose against mine. "Good. Those badgers can—"

A knock on glass interrupts his words and we both look in that direction.

Ember waves from between the slightly open curtain panels. She raises an eyebrow and bites her lip in an expression I know to be lust.

I wave back. "If I'd have known we were going public, I'd have put on more of a show."

Ember shrugs. "It was hard enough not to barge in and join as is." Her voice is muffled from behind the glass wall. She signals behind her to a shocked looking female Seelie with wild red curls. "This is Willow. She's going into Rioch in a couple of days to rescue Kage. We have some questions."

NEXT UP...

Turn the page for a sneak peek of book 3, Willow and King Kage's story, Rescuing the Unseelie King.

Copyright © 2025 by Poppy Minnix

RESCUING THE UNSEELIE KING:

CHAPTER ONE—WIDOW WITH A PLAN

WILLOW

Those Unseelie-eating beasts better be here. I wouldn't have agreed to rescue King Kage if I didn't think they were.

But I'm starting to doubt with all this silence. Rioch is nice enough for a forest territory, though I prefer areas with more open fields lined with an array of flowers instead of the same four types of trees on repeat. Plus, it's easier to see danger in open spaces.

The dryads ignore me from their homes within pines and firs, and, so far, no hellhounds have presented themselves. It's a rumor that the nymphs are using the creatures as guards since they detained the king of the Unseelie Crown Court, but all my hope rides on their presence. Murdering an Unseelie is not something I'm likely to be capable of doing. I only wish for it to be done.

The hole in my heart still gapes for my mate. Flint had been out of the territory at the time and most Seelie are homebodies, only wishing to occupy their areas in peace. If a life is taken outside the defended region... well, they shouldn't have left. Those who believe that didn't lose a mate though, did they?

I still cannot believe Princess Ember bonded with one of them during our traditional Unseelie event, the Springfest Sprint. That was a true slap in the face—not that she understood how much it pained me. So few do.

And now the royals set up a portal for easier travel between the territories. As if there wasn't spilt blood between us. As if I've forgotten what their king did.

But there was a shining bright gem among the muck of that moment, because when the Unseelie announced his name—Prince Typhon Redrek Jenderos—I knew fate had given me an opportunity to ease the pain that has strangled me for so many cycles.

Jenderos.

A prince of the Crown Court provided a link to my worst enemy, his brother, as if determined by fate. I could have laughed if it wouldn't have alerted the crowd that something was terribly off about me. My epiphany unveiled a plan, though I've kept quiet out of necessity.

My people would have stopped me.

The Unseelie would have killed me as they did my mate, instead of welcoming me into their Keep for the past moon—letting the harmless Seelie widow learn their strengths and weaknesses. They trust me. Foolish for fae, but I did good work. And now I will finally gain justice for my slain mate.

Rubbing at my chest doesn't make the tension go away.

And then the most blessed sound fills the forest. A screechy growl. Another farther off.

I grin and perch on a tree.

The creatures wander like beige, furless panthers among the under-brush. No wonder I've had no run-ins with birds, snakes, or even come across a beetle or dragonfly. All creatures have holed themselves away protectively in their hiding spots because death looms on the forest floor.

Perfect.

Now, I only need to get the king out of the nymph coven, remove whatever protection they've given him, and the beasts will take care of my retribution.

"What pretty monsters you are," I whisper when one turns a wild, orange eye on me.

It snorts and continues on.

The Unseelie were right. I'm safe here. Assumed good and gentle. Here to help my grieving process. I've grieved. And all that's left to heal my heart is revenge. Then maybe I'll see a different future from the one I lost.

It was supposed to be easy after Flint and I bonded. My family finally looked at me with something that could be considered pride. I'd found my life's path—had my existence laid out among fields of flowers, mead socials, and children I would have loved far more than I was.

That is all gone because of a king with too much power. It's still so surreal.

Dropping from the tree branch, I flit toward where the main coven building should be, according to the map I memorized. Sure enough, the thatched roof stands out inside a grouping of small huts, stone buildings, and holly bushes.

My target lies within. If I'm very lucky, maybe the king will already be dead.

About the Author

Poppy Minnix

Poppy Minnix is an award-winning author of mythology romantasy and contemporary romance. She loves to reimagine the world with ancient myths present, then dash in some spice and humor. Her characters are hot messes who find their perfect fit in life and in romance. You will find an escape, hidden strength, intriguing and diverse characters, and overcoming shame or guilt in her books.

She lives in Maryland with a husband who is far more romantic than she is, kids, pets, and plants—everything she immensely loves.

Find more about her on socials and her newsletter.

Poppy Minnix
www.poppyminnix.com
poppymwrites@gmail.com

Acknowledgements

Thanks to all the readers who asked for more faetales; there is much more to come and your excitement keeps me writing.

Lori! You're a ball of joyous support. Thank you for your art, reading my works, and your endless positivity. You rock so much!

To Olive. You stood by me—usually on my feet—during every moment of this book's process. Your obsessive doggie stares really held me accountable for getting those words down. I love being your emotional support human.

My family knows I appreciate them, because I say it all the time, but now the world does too. They're supportive and helpful, and I wouldn't be traveling this path without them.